Steven Carroll was born in Melbourne. His first novel, *Remember Me, Jimmy James*, was published in 1992. *The Art of the Engine Driver* (2001) and *The Gift of Speed* (2004) were shortlisted for the Miles Franklin Award, which the final book in the trilogy, *The Time We Have Taken*, won in 2008. Steven Carroll lives in Melbourne with his partner and son.

Praise for Steven Carroll

Highly Commended for the Fellowship of Australian Writers National Literary Awards, 2005

'Exquisite . . . There are times in this book where I paused to admire the subtle craft of what Carroll is doing. Every piece of this book is sanded and planed and perfectly joined. . . Rarely has such an arid place as suburban Melbourne in the heat of 1961 evoked such graceful and tender prose'

The Age

'It is the tender awareness he has of human frailty which lifts the spirit and implores us to simply think better of others and ourselves . . . Carroll writes like a bird freed from a cage. Feeling the pulse of the words with each sentence, the novel has a great current of melancholia coursing through it'

West Australian

'A novel of tender and harro⟨   ⟩*rvateur*

The Gift Of Speed

Steven Carroll

WINDMILL BOOKS

Published by Windmill Books 2011

2 4 6 8 10 9 7 5 3 1

Copyright © Steven Carroll 2004

Steven Carroll has asserted his right under the Copyright, Designs and
Patents Act, 1988, to be identified as the author of this work.

First published in Australia in 2004 by HarperCollins*Publishers*

Windmill Books
The Random House Group Limited
20 Vauxhall Bridge Road, London SW1V 2SA

Addresses for companies within The Random House Group Limited can be found at:
www.randomhouse.co.uk/offices.htm

The Random House Group Limited Reg. No. 954009

www.randomhouse.co.uk

A CIP catalogue record for this book
is available from the British Library

ISBN 9780099537281

The Random House Group Limited supports The Forest Stewardship
Council® (FSC®), the leading international forest certification organisation.
All our titles that are printed on Greenpeace approved FSC® certified paper carry
the FSC® logo. Our paper procurement policy can be found at:
www.randomhouse.co.uk/environment

Printed and bound in Great Britain by
CPI Cox & Wyman, Reading, RG1 8EX

To Leo

Contents

PART FIVE

PART SIX

FINALE

THE GIFT OF SPEED

Part One

21ST–22ND October 1960

The *Strathaird* Docks in Perth

The *Strathaird* glows on the television screen, shimmering on the water the way things from faraway places do, for it has the look of a boat that has come a long way to be here. Michael, currently sprawled on the floor in front of the television, doesn't know how long it takes to cross the world, but it is possible that the *Strathaird* has been travelling all through the winter just to be here for the spring. It is even possible that it brought the sun. It has power and grace and it moves through the water as if barely touching it.

A small pilot craft goes out to greet it and the passengers look down from the high decks of the liner and wave at the toy on the water below. All the time a crowd moves restlessly about on the dock. In the balmy mid-spring, they are dressed in suits and hats, starched shirts, ties, dresses and frocks. And this is something else that Michael notes about this boat — it has the power to bring people out of their houses. These people have left the ease and comfort of their lounge rooms and kitchens and backyards. They may have travelled a long way to greet it. But they have all recognised that this is a boat that deserves to be greeted, one that commands a welcome. For it announces itself, the way important people are announced when they walk into a room. With the smoke from its funnels curling into the morning sky and its horn echoing across the docks, it is acknowledged by everybody around that this is an event. This boat brings with it the spring, summer and autumn sun. It brings music and laughter. It brings with it the cricket.

The players, whose names and records he has studied again and again, are on that boat. Or were, since this is the evening and the events he is watching took place that morning. They are on land. They are here. In a swollen exercise book that should contain school work is a list of all the players in the touring side, with photographs, cut-outs from newspapers and magazines all pasted in, along with quotes and descriptions carefully written beside them. As he compiled the book, Michael came to know the side more and more. And with familiarity, came affection.

Until a part of Michael was drawn to the thought of playing *with* this side, not against it. But they are the opposition and so he has dossiers on every player, noting their strengths and weaknesses, as if, indeed, he were about to play against them. Which is not far from the truth. There will be two series played this season, the one out there on the grounds of Melbourne, Sydney, Brisbane and Adelaide, and the one played inside Michael's head. He knows how he would bowl to Worrell, Sobers and Alexander. And so when he sees their photographs in the newspapers over the following weeks or sees them on the television during the evening news, he will already have a feel for them in the same way that some detectives know their suspects, or the way generals know their opposite number.

A worn cork cricket ball revolves in Michael's fingers as he sits now in his room. He spins it into the air then catches it. Again and again he watches the ball revolve in the air and wonders if — somewhere out there — the fingers of another hand are idly tossing his little world into the air and watching it spin through the heavens of another room. And beyond that the idle fingers of another hand, and another. It goes on forever, worlds within worlds, it's all distinctly possible in Michael's sixteen-year-old mind — and all somewhere out there beyond this pancake suburb.

Numbers, a voice comes back to him from earlier in the day. *Numbers*. And Michael pictures the lean, thin, bony face to which the voice belongs. Numbers, this voice is saying, are the perfect language. The speaker turns from the blackboard — figures and equations etched into every spare space — and smiles as he speaks. But it is the smile, it always seems to Michael, of a torturer or someone who collects insects for the pleasure and satisfaction of pinning them down. The perfect language, his mathematics teacher says again, the same smile still on his face. He knows that nothing he says means anything to the roomful of blank faces staring back at him. He is speaking to the class, but he is really thinking out loud, for his own amusement. When he says that numbers are the perfect language, he slows down as he always does for his good lines. He rarely leaves the blackboard as he scribbles equations on it, pausing to admire them in the same way that the art teacher pauses to admire the coloured slides of famous paintings in the art room.

'Perfect,' he says. 'Absolute precision.'

He then pauses and inspects the faces in the classroom before him, row by row, the smile never leaving his thin lips. But there is no smile in his eyes. His eyes are glancing from face to face and it seems that he is on the point of pinning one of his insects down with a question, but he doesn't and the room relaxes when he goes on.

'We're not talking sums here. We're not talking arithmetic,' and he accents each syllable. 'No, if you're good — any of you — you'll go beyond all that. And you'll know when you've gone beyond all that when the numbers look perfect, and you can see beauty in equations.'

And it is at this point that Michael starts to listen. Not simply look as if he is listening, but really listening. He knows nothing of numbers or equations or figures but he knows what his teacher means, for the idea of perfection had entered Michael's mind long before. The idea that something can be done with such precision that it becomes perfect, and beautiful, is not strange to him. The perfect language. The perfect ball. The ball that Michael will one day bowl. The ball that will become known all across the suburb as the ball that Michael bowled. It is all the same. And if they are the same he will know he is getting somewhere when the rhythm of his run, the stretch of his delivery stride, the roll of his arm and the sight of the ball moving through the air all become beautiful.

That afternoon, when the classrooms had emptied and everybody was home, he went to the wire nets of the school that was once Skinner's farm, and bowled his worn cork cricket ball as he does every day after school. And each time he bowled he waited for that moment of perfection — like the perfect equation in the perfect language — to pass through him. Perhaps just a hint of it was all he wanted, just to know it could be done. But he never felt it. Not once. Today he was ugly. Today he was disgusted with himself. And so he bowled for longer than he usually would, to get the ugliness out of him. But it didn't go and he walked home exhausted. He slumped onto the floor in the lounge room and said nothing to anyone. Then he looked up and that was when he saw the boat.

He has left the lounge room now; his parents, Vic and Rita, are talking quietly in the kitchen, and that luminous boat has long since faded from the television screen. He throws the ball into the air and watches it spin. Then he drops it onto his bed and steps out of his room and into the backyard. The flyscreen door snaps behind him in the night. The branches of the plum tree stoop to the ground, brushing the lawn. The apricots, passionfruit and lemons are all on the way. Above him the night sky is clear and wide. The moon sails through occasional puffs of cloud. At the bottom of the yard he can see the three white stumps painted on the fence, then he glances back up at the sky, half-expecting to see that boat sailing towards him through the Milky Way.

Then his yard is no longer his yard, but a vast green playing field. It is neither day nor night. The green of the field is deep and the white clothes of the players standing upon it glow in the half-light. They do not notice Michael. They are playing cricket. They are intent on what they are doing. There is a low, white wooden fence surrounding the oval and the only way onto the playing field is through a small gate in front of him. The gate is closed and he knows that it will only open for him if he has the gift of speed. And if he does, if he can bring that gift with him, then the gate will open at the lightest touch, and he will join that company already gathered out there on the playing field. But for the moment he can only stand and watch. The players on the field do not notice him. They are intent on what they are doing. They are playing cricket.

2.

French Windows

T he next day a builder visits the house. His plans are laid out on the lawn, secured with a couple of empty teacups. The plans are simple, easy to follow, as the builder explains them to Vic and Rita. At first the builder addresses himself to Vic, but it doesn't take long before he turns to Rita.

It is early afternoon. Vic's golf buggy and clubs are in the driveway. He is eager to leave and isn't concentrating, besides he's got the picture. The broad picture. Rita wants the details. A light breeze rattles the new green leaves of the silver birch in the centre of the lawn, and the sun plays on them like it would on water, the green waves of new foliage gently rising and falling. It is a perfect day to be out on the fairway and Vic has stepped back from the conversation like a man who has already handed over any say in the whole business.

Rita wants the details. The builder rises from the plans, ignoring Vic by now (and Vic is happy to be ignored), and walks towards the lounge-room wall. He looks back at Rita still standing on the lawn, points to the frame of the lounge-room window, then draws an imaginary vertical line all the way down to the ground. He does the same for the frame on the other side.

'Nothing to it,' he says, standing by the window. 'Like slicing bread.'

Rita and Vic nod as the builder speaks. But they are different nods. Rita is nodding with a slight squint. In a simple, yellow summer dress, she is looking hard at the front of her house, imagining what the new windows will look like. It is a nod of involvement. She is a study in concentration. Vic is nodding like a man who is already standing on the first tee. His gaze takes in the bright, white weatherboards of the house, the window, the builder, but his mind is elsewhere. He doesn't need to look any more. He's got the picture. They're getting French windows. He knows what that means. Fancy little numbers. Like they have in fancy little French villages in those magazines Rita buys that put all sorts of fancy ideas in people's minds — like sticking up French windows where there's already perfectly good ones. And, there *will* be lace, there will be curtains. There might even be shutters, for Christ's sake. Little white shutters, and long windows that open out onto the street like doors. And, in the end, that's where the idea falls down, he thinks, nodding to himself. You can put up as many French windows as you like — and you can sit behind them and imagine you're in some cosy, colourful French village and not the dull, flat place you've got no choice but to call home — but those windows, however fancy, are always going to open out onto the street. And, of course, the street is going to look back at the French windows and nod knowingly. Her — they will say — her doing. And they'll be right, because the windows have Rita's name written all over them. Just like her dresses, these windows are a bit too good for the street. And the street doesn't like that. And already, he's feeling just a bit embarrassed about the whole caper, because he knows it will be a conversation piece. The street will talk about the changes to the house and he will be called upon to explain all this to his neighbours, for, unlike Rita, Vic knows the neighbourhood and talks to them. It will happen. And just as Vic did when Rita first raised the matter the street will hear a new term: French windows. And the very word 'French' will have them all nodding. And they will, no doubt, all of them, look about their street in such a way as to suggest that French windows might be all right in France, but this isn't France. Vic will read these sentiments in their eyes and whoever, whichever one of his neighbours he may be speaking to at the time will nod slowly, again and again, repeating the phrase that he or she has just learnt: French windows.

It was the same with his mother's piano, back there in that poky little hole in South Melbourne, years ago before his mother followed them up to the country where she still lives. The best room in that poky little hole was barely big enough for a couple of armchairs, but she insisted on having a piano. She paid it off week by week for years. Not that she could play it. Not that he could. Nobody could. Not a note. But she polished it and cleaned it. And every year she brought the tuner in. And when his friends dropped by they'd see it standing up there in the best room, dominating a whole wall like some cathedral organ come down in the world, and they'd say to Vic, 'C'mon then, gives us a tune.' But Vic couldn't play it. And then they'd say, 'Well, c'mon, Mrs C, you give us a tune.' But she couldn't and neither could any of his mates. And so they all had a chuckle about that, every time. It was a running joke. But everybody agreed it was a wonderful piece of work. 'German,' his mother would say, her eyes falling fondly on the instrument, completely untroubled by the fact that it had never been played. Still, she kept it tuned, in case some day, someone dropped in who could play and the house would ring with the sound.

The builder takes three paces forward and Vic returns to the present. The builder then draws an imaginary line across the lawn with his foot.

'There, that's where it reaches to.'

'Where what reaches to?' says Vic.

The builder looks up at him as if having completely forgotten he was there.

'The patio,' says Rita, as if it were obvious.

'Patio?'

Vic knows nothing about this and he thinks about going on with it, but Rita shoots him a quick look and he drops it. Besides, the look she shot him was probably right. 'That's what you get,' it said, 'for not listening.' But, even so, as the builder paces it out this patio is starting to look enormous and already he is starting to wonder how he can explain *this* to the street.

Soon the builder rolls his rough plans up and Vic is free to go. But before he does Rita turns to him.

'Well?'

'Looks good,' he says. 'Big,' he adds, in that special way he has of using the word 'big' — meaning special. Grand. Then he grins.

The wheels of his buggy crunch on the gravel of the driveway. From the driveway entrance he sees the rotted golf-course gate through which the great Arnie Palmer strode the previous spring. The great Arnie Palmer, who had the even, glowing tan of an American god come to town and a smile that came from a lifetime of teeing off on crisp, brilliant mornings, with the dew still under your feet. And with the tan, and the smile, came the kind of golfing cardigan you just couldn't buy here. Not that Vic would want one. Cardigans like that belong to the Arnie Palmers of this world, not weekday pretenders. It is a short walk to this broken gate that is now sacred. Vic takes in the gums, the direction of the wind, and Rita can tell he's happy. He waves briefly as he leaves. He's happy, all right. It's always the same. He always looks happiest when he's leaving. And his walk is the same as it always has been. His body leaning forward as if labouring into a chilly wind. A winter walk in summer.

The builder hands her the rolled-up plans and soon Rita is alone in the middle of the lawn holding onto the plans and admiring the house as if the windows were already there.

She knows what they all think — Vic, the neighbours, the street. The damned, bloody stupid street. Well, she thinks, this will give them something to talk about. What does she care for the street anyway? She barely talks to anybody. The trees are starting to grow and the tarred roads and concrete footpaths have made a difference, but this place will always remain a backwater. She will always remember the street the way it was when they first came to it — raw and exposed. Bare wooden houses, bare muddy blocks and barking dogs — like something out of the Dark Ages. It's a hot afternoon but she shivers at the memory of it then turns back to the house and notes that it doesn't look too bad. White. There's nothing like a white house. She always wanted a white house and now she has one. The street might not be the end of the world as it once was, when she felt that if she weren't careful walking back from the station on dark nights — and they were always dark because there were no streetlights — when she felt that if she strayed from her usual path she could easily fall off the edge of the earth altogether. She would forever be dragging the street after her. She couldn't change any of that, or Vic, for that matter, but she could change the house. And when she came back at nights after work she would have something to contemplate now on the walk home from the station. When the job is done, the fresh white paint will gleam under the garden light — because a garden must have a light, just as a house must be illuminated when viewed from the street. The new windows, the brass fittings, the painted patio, will all be waiting for her, sparkling in the night so that anybody passing in the street will pause to look.

3.

A Players' Chorus

While Rita is contemplating the front of the house and Vic is striding towards the golf course, Michael hears music. At first it is soft, like a whisper. Then it is stronger, sweeping across the dried playing fields of the school with the dusty north wind. Soon it fills the room and he wonders why the quiet activity of the classroom hasn't been disturbed. But nobody lifts their head and Michael doodles on the page in front of him as a symphony of metal drums and island voices drowns out the morning.

Before every game they play this calypso music. He's read this. They gather in a room, turn on the hi-fi, and the sound of tin drums and steel guitars fills the air for an hour before play. Both teams sing these songs together. And he can see them tapping their feet, singing, moving to the rhythms of the music he hears on the radio because this summer has brought them all more than just cricket. Sobers, Davidson, Kanhai, McDonald — the great Hall — they all gather before the games and listen to the same songs. He can imagine Sobers dancing to this music in the rooms that overlook the grounds upon which the series will be played. Sobers plays like a dancer, light on his feet, skipping down the pitch, this music possibly going through one part of his mind while that part of his mind that plays cricket can get on with the business at hand without too much conscious effort. And perhaps Davidson, whose job it will be to stop the dancing Sobers, perhaps he too has this music rolling round somewhere at the back of his mind as his right arm rises and he sights the stumps through the crook in his elbow, sees the batsman's pads, and eyes the exact spot he wants the ball to land as his left arm whips over and the ball begins its swinging, cutting journey to Sobers at the other end of the pitch. Sobers, who — at that moment of imagined delivery — may well be inwardly humming the very same chorus that Davidson is. They may each be humming exactly the same line — same words, same melodic strain — in that split second it takes for the ball to leave Davidson's hand and reach Sobers's bat, or beat it. Is this also the music that the great Hall hears as he runs to the bowling crease? Is this what he will hear as he runs in again and again throughout the summer? In the First Test the great Hall will run up to the bowling crease and bowl three hundred and sixty-eight times. He will run miles and miles, in short sprints.

With the music still in his ears, Michael picks up his ballpoint pen — the one his English teacher says is good only for inferior words. Serious words, he says, need to be written with a fountain pen. Serious words will only respect the nib and ink of a proper pen, not the insult of an American ballpoint. Nonetheless, Michael picks up his ballpoint pen and begins his calculations. The great Hall bowls forty overs a match. If he bowls three hundred and twenty times, he covers ten miles simply by running in to bowl. But it is not simply the numbers, nor the speed. It is the way Hall bowls. He bowls like this music — loud, bright and brash. He brings laughter to bowling. It is a different kind of bowling altogether from the great Lindwall, who was cool and smooth, and not only had the gift of speed but the gift of grace. To watch the great Lindwall bowl was to marvel that anybody could do that. There are those, Michael knows, who say that he learnt from the great Larwood, and there are those who say he was simply blessed and could bowl like that before he could walk. Throughout the summer, and the summers to follow, Michael will return to the action of the great Lindwall and indeed marvel that anybody could do that. And he will eventually come to the only conclusion that makes sense, the only conclusion there is. That the great Lindwall had no idea how he got it himself, because it was a gift. He ran in to bowl one day and discovered — quite casually — that he had this thing, this gift. And his life from then on would be lived in its light and its shadow.

But the gift of speed comes in different ways. Michael cannot imagine music in the great Lindwall's ears as he swoops upon the bowling crease. But he can in the great Hall's. And when he reaches his delivery stride does the batsman at the other end hear the sound of metal drums and island voices? Is it just possible that the music they all share in the mornings before these state and country matches in the players' rooms, stays with them out on the field? That when the great Hall runs towards the pitch, those who wait — the batsman at the other end, the fieldsmen — share this music? And is it possible that in the quiet moments, when the damage has been done, when the stings from being struck have dulled to an ache and the great Hall is walking back to his bowling mark, that they all return to this music they shared before the game, and that one, or two, or all of the players in the lull between deliveries, hear exactly the same chorus, exactly the same lines at exactly the same moment, and that at such times a symphony of metal drums and island voices engulfs the playing field?

4.

On the Fairway

At the same time that Rita is contemplating the front of the house where the new French windows will go, and while Michael sits in his classroom listening to the island symphony, Vic is on the fairway.

The world is wide again out here. No houses, no streets, no footpaths. Nothing but the endless fairway rolled out before him. Crisp, trimmed and springy as a new carpet beneath his feet, the bright green lawns sweep down the gradual slope of the first fairway until the grass meets the creek that once ran through the whole suburb. Once children jumped this creek going to and from school, now it runs unseen and unheard beneath the footpaths and roads of the suburb. On the other side of the creek the fairway starts again and runs up to the meticulously manicured green where a small red flag flutters in the afternoon breeze.

You need binoculars to see that far, binoculars strong enough to see into the future because that's where that tiny red triangle of fluttering red cloth seems to be. You also need a good, strong swing to hit the ball that far. The first tee of this golf course is famous across the city. A few minutes ago, as Vic stood on the tee, his legs perfectly placed, his balance just right and the glistening white ball firmly in his sights, he felt as though he might be able to hit that ball clear into tomorrow. And when he hit the ball he was sure he had never hit a ball so cleanly and sweetly before in his life. But the stroke was no match for the fairway and it landed a brisk stroll away. One day he'll look up and that ball really will be a tiny, white dot on a distant green.

As he dropped his club back into the bag, Vic and the three other men with whom he has teamed up for the afternoon began their stroll out to the middle of the fairway, and that was when the world opened up and he forgot all about the shot and his disappointment. The green and white clubhouse shrank behind them, the foursome waiting on the tee to play next became small and the world became wide again. Wide, like it always was when he drove those old engines all through the night, clear out into the next morning. Like it always was when he drove out into the sun with the whole city spread out in front of him and everybody was still sleeping. And because he'd seen tomorrow rise up before him time and again on the night shift, he never doubted that tomorrow would always be there to be driven into and that the world would always be wide. That was the kind of expectation that engine driving gave you.

He wheels his buggy down to where his ball lies and watches as, one by one, the other three players clip their balls across the creek. He knows one of them, Gannon, an ex-policeman, a short, square man, but he doesn't know the other two. Gannon is graceless and brutal. He clubs the ball, bludgeons it onward and the ball resists him, but goes anyway, on pain of further violence. Another, an accountant in a neatly ironed golf shirt and yellow leather gloves, is a morning golfer whose day has been thrown out. As Vic studies him, he can see that he has the crisply dressed look of a man used to teeing off with the dew beneath his feet, just like Arnie. The third is a bank manager who slips away from his office once a week. Out here they all cease to be what they were and are — an ex-engine driver, an ex-detective, an accountant and a bank manager. Out here, they are golfers.

Nobody says much. Vic watches as the new, white balls, each in turn, glide across the creek and land within chipping distance of the green, its flag still fluttering in the afternoon breeze. Beyond the fairway, the rough, the ghost gums, pines and the rotted wooden fence that runs along the eastern boundary of the golf course, the rest of the world goes on. Somewhere out there, Webster's factory presses scrap metal into spare engine parts; special wheat trains bring grain to the mill; Nat, the Italian barber, trims a customer's moustache; a red suburban rattler pulls out of the station; and Bruchner's builders raise a wooden beam into place on the square frame that will be somebody's home.

The quiet, weekday industry of the suburb continues as it always does, nobody looking up. Vic sweeps on up the fairway. He feels the breeze on his cheek — and after a lifetime of shaving twice before work he feels that breeze more keenly than those around him. As he turns his cheek to the side to feel the full rush of the breeze part of him is driving again. And as he steps over the small, wooden bridge that fords the creek, he looks around him at the sky and the tall gums that were all there before the suburb arrived, and briefly recovers that feeling of width that his world once had.

5.

Webster's Factory

Michael is carrying his school bag over his shoulder on his walk home. His usual way does not require him to cross the railway line — there are really two suburbs — his side of the railway line and the other side, east and west. And whenever he crosses the railway line he feels, for that time, out of his territory. But this afternoon he has been distracted by the sight of Webster's factory.

This whole block, this acre of open ground bordered by the railway line and the two main streets of the suburb has always been vacant, flat ground, for as long as he can remember. But during the last few months it has taken on the appearance of a battlefield. Not that Michael has ever seen one.

The machines from Webster's factory have been tipped out into the open. All of them. And the mystery of the factory, the mystery of what goes on inside, is now in plain view for everyone to see. Webster's was the first factory in the suburb. It takes up a whole block. A long, red brick building with the name Webster in high metal lettering at the front as if it were a department store and not a factory. The owner of the factory is simply known in the area as Webster. Nothing more. He is not referred to by his other names because no one seems to know them. Nor is he referred to as Mr Webster. He is simply Webster of Webster's factory. He is his factory. His factory is him. And so — to the people of the suburb, those employed in his factory — he is simply Webster. The way, it occurs to Michael, that you would talk about Larwood or Jardine. Their surnames are enough and no one thinks to place a Christian name or a Mr before Webster. It is a name written in metal at the front of the factory. Nothing else is required.

Mulling over this Michael wanders through the rows of discarded machines in the paddock. Already rusted by the spring rain, but with the smell of oil hanging about them from the days when they pressed scrap metal into spare engine parts, these machines have a military look. Like tanks and cannons from jungle battles that might just as easily have been fought on the golf course, for the war in this suburb is never far away. Every day, to and from school, he passes the house of Hacker Paine. Hacker Paine, who never returned from the war quite right, who is often to be found on the golf course on summer nights, patrolling the undergrowth for the remnants of an Imperial Japanese Army that had surrendered years before but which is forever invading his sleep. Hacker Paine — teacher, war hero — whose shoulders spanned the Grade Five doorway, whose medals jangled in the corridors of the school every Anzac Day, whose only daughter lost her head when her sports car ran under a semi-trailer parked on the dark highway out beyond the suburb on the hill called Pretty Sally — Hacker Paine is never at rest. And the war that he brought back with him is never far away in this suburb.

It is late afternoon and the rust that covers the machines is the same bright orange as the sun that now coats the corrugated iron of the factory roof. Levers and plunges and giant hammers that crush and flatten are all around him in shadow and light. Giant wheels with metal teeth have rusted into place where they last stopped. These levers and hammers could crush limbs with the same indifference that they crushed sheet metal. And those giant wheels with metal teeth could chew up fingers and hands in a flash if you were unlucky enough to get your hands in the way — and it occurs to Michael as he stares at the machines that hands and limbs would surely have been crushed and chewed up by these things.

He comes to a large pressing machine which is near the back of the factory and must have been protected from the rain because it's not cloaked in rust and the smell of lubricating oil is still strong. It looks like it still works. Looks as if it were used just yesterday, as if it could be used right now. The metal is blue and shiny and greased — ready. Michael looks about the block, from the rows of piled metal to the red brick wall of the factory, and sees nobody.

He steps up to the platform where a machine worker would, until recently, have stood all day, repeating the same actions over and over again. With his bowling arm he reaches out for the handle that controls the wheel, that turns the wheel, that lowers the hammer that does the crushing. He pauses before deciding to set the thing in motion — then turns the handle. It moves easily, like the wheel of a small bicycle, and at once all the other parts of the machine that he hadn't even noticed until now snap into operation. The whole apparatus responds to his fingertips, as wheels with blue metal teeth turn more wheels and the hammer suddenly drops and crushes non-existent scrap and Michael jumps back as if he has set off a bomb. He looks about but not even the birds in the trees along the street have stirred. It must surely have been so thunderous that the whole neighbourhood heard. But no one has. So, with nobody about and nobody looking on, he steps back up to the machine and sets the whole thing in motion again. The hammer springs into place and Michael notices a metal can on the ground next to the machine. It is a strong looking can, more like a container, one that once housed tea or biscuits. He picks it up, wondering what impact the hammer would have, curious to know just what this hammer can do if given something to crush.

With the can in hand, he reaches his bowling arm out across the machine towards the spot where the hammer hits, leaves the can there, then hurriedly removes his hand. Wheels turn wheels, and the hammer pounds into the can and crushes it flat in an instant, then springs back into place awaiting further instructions. Michael retrieves the can from the machine. As he turns it in his fingers he realises that it has not been crushed flat, that the can was larger, wider than the hammer, that there is a rim all around it and what was once a can now resembles a small bowl. Or, and he reappraises his first impression, an ashtray. He has, he now decides, just manufactured an ashtray. The faded paint that covered the original can is still visible and the whole thing is good to look at. He can, with no difficulty, see it sitting on the coffee table in their lounge room and he decides on the spot that he will take it home and give it to his father as a gift.

Pleased with himself he doesn't at first notice the back double doors of the factory open, but something catches his attention and he turns to see two men standing in the doorway. He slips the crushed can into his pocket and begins walking back along the row of discarded and rusted machines that eventually leads back out onto the road. He turns once. One of the men is short and square and compact — as if crushed into shape by Webster's machines. The other is tall, his hair is grey at the sides, and his legs are planted on the factory floor as if having taken root there. He is wearing a dark brown suit and blowing smoke into the air as he laughs. Although he has never seen him, this — Michael knows — is Webster.

And in the instant that Michael turns, Webster looks up from his conversation and sees him making his way out — a kid, no doubt, who's just been up to no good, like most of the kids in this suburb. But Webster does nothing, his eyes see Michael off his property, and he returns to his conversation with the short, squat man who looks to have been crushed into shape by one of his machines.

* * *

With his house calls completed, at the wheel of the Land Rover he has become famous for, Dr Peter Black waits for the lights at Webster's corner, noting young Michael to his right, the boy's school bag over his shoulder as he emerges from the factory. He knows Michael. He knows the whole family. More, he suspects, than the family knows itself. Vic already has a dodgy heart from the years of hard living and Black has told him time and again to give up the booze or the pills he takes will be useless. But the prospect of death does not bother the boy's father, Black muses as Michael steps out onto the street. Most people fear the Distinguished Guest, but not Vic. He is, Black recognised from the very start, one of those who will live and die in the manner of their own choosing. And it doesn't matter what you tell them. The physician in Black is appalled, the writer he might have become (still curled up inside him) is intrigued.

Black is a Jamesian doctor and it is often said that he bears a striking resemblance to the frog-faced transatlantic American whose complete works he has read over and again. At one stage during his studies literature almost took over, to the point that he nearly threw in medicine and a life in general practice, for the life of the famous literary doctors of the past. But in the end it was never a difficult decision and instead of the writer's life he found himself a practice in a frontier suburb because no one else would go there and because the place needed a doctor. A suburb called, and the doctor in Black, not the writer, answered.

The Distinguished Guest. It is a phrase he delights in and uses often. It was with a shock that he went back to the source one night in the *Oxford Book of Quotations* and discovered that the great master had on his deathbed not referred to the imminent arrival of the Distinguished Guest, but the Distinguished Thing. Thing? It was not a word he would have imagined Mr James ever using. But he had and Black had got it wrong. Or, perhaps he hadn't. Perhaps he had got it right and Mr James had got it wrong. Perhaps the writer in Black the doctor had rejected the word 'thing' in the same way that a body rejects a heart. Gazing through the dusty windscreen he contents himself that it was not so much a travesty as an improvement.

With the change of lights, taking in Michael's bouncing lope and still simultaneously appalled at and intrigued with the nonchalance with which Vic treats the Distinguished Guest, Black continues on his way to his practice at the top of the main street; to his practice, and the life he has chosen, while Webster and one of his workers blow cigarette smoke into the blue, suburban sky.

6.

Frank Worrell Alone

Frank Worrell is alone. On the other side of the country while Michael is departing Webster's factory, Frank Worrell is alone because he wants to be. In the players' room of a private school in Perth, he sits in a cane chair looking out over the playing field at his team in training. A small crowd, mostly schoolchildren and teachers, is gathered round the white boundary fence. He watches his players in the nets. From the faces of his players and this small crowd he can see the signs of laughter and excited talk. And from the silent strokes of his players, he knows that this laughter and this talk will be punctuated by the gentle *clock clock* of bat hitting ball. But he hears none of it. The room in which he sits is sealed. The door is firmly closed, the windows shut. The room is shaded and cool, the afternoon sun is bright. The silent scene outside may as well belong to another world. Frank Worrell is alone, a world unto himself. His fingers drum softly on the long wooden table that runs almost the entire length of the room. Pads, bats, gloves, newspapers, cigarettes and sweet drinks lie on the table, boots and shoes across the floor. But he pays no attention to any of it. Frank Worrell is dressed in his whites ready to join his team, but he doesn't.

He needs to sit. To be alone. And when he is done with sitting and being alone, he will join his team. But not yet. At the moment he is perfectly still in his cane chair. His eyes, unblinking, are fixed on the playing field, his fingers continue to drum softly on the wooden table. You have to strain to hear the sound of his drumming fingers, but it's there — rhythmic, steady, barely touching the surface of the table, as if, instead of a wooden table, his fingers are idly drumming the skin on a bowl of water. The skin is the surface tension that enables a fly to walk on water. And throughout the summer Frank Worrell must learn to think like a fly walking on water. He can make no mistakes or he will break the surface tension that he walks on, and drown. This cricketer must also learn to speak the language of diplomacy. He must learn to speak it quickly and fluently, and he needs to be sure of everything and everyone around him. So he is alone for the moment, in this quiet time before it all begins, in this room shut off from the noise of the world. His mind is working silently, and the only sign that the invisible activity of thinking is taking place is the drumming of his fingers in the hush of the room.

The island politics, the manoeuvrings, the intrigues, the deals — from Antigua to Jamaica, Barbados, Trinidad and Tobago, from which he always remained distant — are all behind him now. The fight is over. The battle has been won. Frank Worrell is captain. The first black man to lead his country. And he feels the weight of it, now, sitting at the table of the players' room of a private school in Perth, his mind moving in silence. He will feel that weight throughout the whole summer. It has come down to him. He is the one who must make it work and the one to whom everyone will turn when difficult decisions have to be made. He accepts it all because it had to come down to someone. All that he asks for at the moment is this quiet time before it all begins, so he can accustom himself to the newness of it, feel it, and silently tell himself to get used to it. To wear this weight as though it is the most natural thing in the world to carry with you every minute of the day and night. To wear it so naturally that nobody notices the weight is upon you. And somewhere inside his head, not worth uttering now, not worth uttering any more because the fight is over and the battle won, is the barely fathomable thought that it took until this summer, this summer of 1960, for it to happen. If there is any anger, it does not show, and it will never show. It doesn't matter now. Frank Worrell is captain. Behind the ever-present sunny smile, the bright eyes, the quick riposte, this weight will be there. And so he sits, still and silent, watching his players through the wide windows of the school's clubhouse rooms. And the question he is asking himself is the same he has often asked since the captaincy passed to him: who is a team man, who is not? It is a concern of utmost significance, more significant even than victory. This is the first question Frank Worrell asks himself when he looks at his players, because Frank Worrell plays for the team, and this summer his team will be playing more than just cricket. The burden of making this thing work has fallen to him and he must know before he even walks onto an arena that the most minute of his directions will be carried out because his players will be team men. And they will show the islands of their home what a team can do. There must be no disagreements on the field, no hint of controversy. No sniff of failure. He must handle this thing, this captaincy, this weight, not as well as everybody else who has gone before him or anybody who might have had his job this summer, but better than anybody else. They will be playing more than cricket this summer and the silent, still figure of Frank Worrell, his fingers drumming the surface of the table ever so softly as he takes in the low, slanting sunshine through the schoolyard elms, knows this.

It is a weight that can't be shared, and so he chooses this quiet moment before everything begins to sit and dwell on what must be done. Frank Worrell is alone. And there is a part of Frank Worrell that will, throughout the summer, remain alone. The part that can't be shared.

When he's done with the sitting and the thinking and his fingers stop their drumming, there is a sudden silence in the room. It is the kind of silence that follows when a sound is so subtle it is only noticed when it ceases. His fingers stop their drumming, he rises from his chair, shakes the stillness from him, and steps out through the club-room door into the bright, afternoon light, the line of the sun touching the tops of the schoolyard elms.

The noise of the world rushes up to him; its urgency, its immediacy, its inescapability. The excited talk, the laughter, the clear, sharp *clock clock* of bat and ball are suddenly upon him and all around him. On the walk down to the playing field, now surrounded by students from the school and members of the public, signing autographs with the sunny smile back on his face and waving to well-wishers, Frank Worrell is alone. And he will stay that way throughout the summer.

7.

The Girls' Home

The Girls' Home is a place of mystery — set back from the street in a world of its own, a world of cast-iron balconies, tall, closed doors and wide grounds upon which no girls play. With its picket fence enclosing the grounds and its front gate shutting the rest of the neighbourhood out, it is a distant building, the most distant in the suburb.

Michael, the crushed tin ashtray from Webster's factory still in his pocket, need not pass the Girls' Home on the way back from school. It is one street further on from the one he would normally take. It is neither on his way nor out of his way, but he is aware of breaking his routine on these afternoons when he does not turn right at the usual street, but walks straight ahead to the new, red brick Catholic

Church at the corner, before turning right and eventually passing the distant windows of the Girls' Home.

And it is not simply that the house is set back from the street that makes it a place of distance and mystery, nor the fact that no girls play on its wide lawns — at least, not when Michael passes. It is also the girls inside.

The Home has always been there. And when it wasn't a Home it was a hospital for returned soldiers and before that somebody's private house. But it has been a Girls' Home for as long as Michael can remember. And in all that time — whenever he had walked or ridden past on his bicycle and observed that long, cast-iron balcony with its wide windows flickering between the trees and shrubs that lined the front fence — he has thought very little about the place, apart from knowing intuitively that it is a place of intrigue. It was always the house where girls who had no parents lived. Those whose parents — and this was a mystery too — were missing. Those whose parents were forever to be marked 'Not Present'. Even though all the students at the school played in the yard and on the ovals together — and Michael has known their faces from his early school years — he has always been aware of the fact that at the end of the day these girls went back to the Home.

When people spoke of the Home it was never in the same way you normally spoke of home, and whenever the girls strolled through the streets of the suburb or wandered the playing field or quadrangles of the schoolyard, they always carried the mystery of the place with them. And they always had that look in their eyes, that they too knew that come the end of the day everybody else went home to their own houses, yards and families while they went back to the Home. As familiar as they might be in the schoolyards and streets, once they stepped inside the front gate of the Home, once they strolled across its wide, open lawns and into the house, they became a mystery again.

Kathleen Marsden is one of those girls who has no parents and lives in the Girls' Home. Michael has known her for many years, although he is not sure how many. At some stage during his life she slipped into the playground, into his classroom and was suddenly there. And he would be aware of her in the same way that he would be aware of the familiar faces in his class — just as part of him would always have been aware that when she left the school she returned to the Home. But nothing more than that.

Now, more often than not, instead of walking back from school the usual way, he walks past the

Home. And there is no particular reason for this change, which is made all the more significant by the fact that Michael is already a boy of habits and routines, someone who likes his routines and rarely changes them. There is nothing that he can point to with conviction and say *that* is why. That is why I walk a new way home. Only a look. A look he observed one day on Kathleen Marsden's face, a smile, not directed at him, but to a friend on the far side of a shelter shed. And not even a recent look, but an old one, a very old one. A quick smile from years before in the days when they all played in shelter sheds on rainy days and the sheds were always crammed and hot and filled with the noise of a hundred voices. A smile from years before that he recalled just a few weeks ago when he was watching her sitting with her friends on the main oval of the high school to which they had both gone. Kathleen Marsden was sitting on the oval with two of her friends, their long winter uniforms spilling over the grass, and that rainy-day smile was suddenly there again on her lips and in her eyes. It was not as though he had deliberately sought her out. No, he had simply turned round for no particular reason and she had been there. And when he saw her he had silently noted that that was Kathleen Marsden and she was smiling. And he thought nothing of it until later in the day when he found himself remembering the same smile from years before when they were children and played in shelter sheds on wet days and hit each other to show their affections. And this memory came as a puzzle because he knew only too well that her smile had not been for him. But at some stage during the afternoon it slowly dawned on him that that was it. What had touched him and stuck to him and lodged in him was just that — that the smile had not been for him. A part of him had silently longed that it had been, and some silent, long-ago longing was only now being registered in his head or his heart or his bones, or whatever part of the body it is that tells people that they long for something and that the bittersweet burden of caring for someone has fallen upon them.

He slows his pace — for it is not speed but slowness that he now wants — as he passes the Home.

It is late in the afternoon, he is looking forward to training at the school nets, hungrily determined to become faster and faster each day. But now, as he passes the Home, he consciously slows his pace. The slowness he adopts, and which doesn't come naturally, allows him the chance of catching a glimpse of her. The windows from the balcony of the Home are half up to let the breeze through. They would all be in there, but no talk carries to him — the Home is too far from the street for talk to be heard — and there is no laughter. Nothing loud that might disturb the quiet mystery of the place. But he knows that Kathleen Marsden is in there, behind one of those half-opened windows, in one of those quiet rooms. Doing something, or simply doing nothing.

8.

In the Nets

There it is, the only sound that has ever mattered. Speed. Summer has not yet come to the suburb and the afternoons have not yet become endless. For an hour now he has been bowling in the concrete and wire cricket nets. Already the light is fading, and soon it will be too difficult to bowl, for the transition from half-light to darkness is still swift, like it is in winter. Not that he hasn't bowled in the dark. Not that he hasn't bowled when it has been so dark that he may as well have been bowling blind. Soon, this half-light will be gone, he will make the short walk home, and the best part of the day will be over.

Tomorrow he will once again return to that forgetful world of rhythm and speed, to the oblivion of bowling. At all other times of the day or night he is either looking forward or looking back, but not in the nets. In the nets time ceases to matter and it is only the fading light that tells him that somewhere out there in the everyday world time is, in fact, passing. The light, and the six o'clock bells of St Matthew's tell him this. But, even so, those bells and that fading light both belong to another world. The sun sinks on other people's days, the bells of St Matthew's ring for other people's ears. Not his. Not in the nets.

This is the part of the day that belongs to him entirely. And those instruments that measure the passing of time and the day, all those daily occurrences that mark the passage of the hours such as lunch, the last lesson and the seven o'clock news, don't matter here. And when the last ball is bowled, when he steps back into the everyday life of the suburb, he always has the feeling of stepping back into some foreign world that was never meant for him and which has merely claimed him again for the time being.

As he walks home along the illuminated bitumen streets to his house, the ball still in hand, his school bag over his shoulder, he dwells on the summer that will soon be upon them — the cricket, the end of school and the long, warm evenings to come — and he is already looking forward to it all, just as, by the end of the summer, he will be looking back on it all. The time in the nets, that wasn't time at all, is gone.

The lights of the golf-course clubhouse shine brightly to his left. Inside, their faces red from the sun, the last of the weekday golfers will be at the bar filling up as quickly as possible before returning home, not enough presence of mind left in them to know that the time for coming and going has already passed and that they are in that curious state of being drunk before they know it. He hears the occasional sounds of motor cars along the main road behind him, sees the bare frames of new houses popping up on the few vacant blocks that remain, while overhead an aeroplane drones across the suburb, its lights quickly fading into the darkness.

Beyond the golf-course clubhouse, the ghost gums, the ferns and the low pines that line the eastern fence of the course, stand silently watching everything — slow, steady growers in a puzzling world of speed.

Part Two

14TH–31ST December 1960
2ND January 1961

9.

Lindsay Hassett's Sports Store

Michael has just left the gaping mouth of Flinders Street Station behind him. In the cool arcades of the city, in the shaded lanes and in the 'little' streets that parallel the major ones, everybody has taken off their coats and cardigans and loosened their ties. It is cool in the arcades, but it is coolest in the basement shops that run off them.

The lunch-time crowd moves all around him, but Michael doesn't notice them. He is lingering at the shop sign in front of him that says *Lindsay Hassett's Sports Store*, before following the arrow that points down into the cool depths of the basement shop. He always pauses before this sign, always waits that second or two before descending.

Everything he would one day need is in this shop. To be a proper cricketer — like the cricketers in the books and newspapers, in magazines and on the television — he would need to look like one. And everything he would need to acquire that look is in this shop. All the other shops are inferior, they sell inferior goods. But here everything is as it should be.

It is a busy shop, but a quiet one. Nobody speaks loudly. People rarely speak above a whisper, as though they were in an art gallery or a library. And from time to time, the crisp, dry, quiet voice of Hassett himself can be heard as he slowly moves about the shop inquiring if his customers need anything or if he can help them in any way. And when he isn't speaking to his customers he is talking cricket — with players, old and new, visiting the shop — in that voice Michael knows from the radio. Here the air is crowded with talk of cricket, by those who not only know their cricket but know how to talk about it. Michael knows his cricket, but he keeps quiet here and listens and watches.

Hassett is not a big man nor is he loud. Every time Michael visits the shop Hassett seems to look more like a writer than a cricketer, like someone who has made his name with a pen and typewriter instead of a bat and pads. Like someone who has spent the years tapping out words, not runs, someone who amassed books not centuries —

someone who might even find a cricket ball, hurled at sufficient pace, a trifle disconcerting as they might say in the types of books and plays he imagines Hassett, the writer, writing. And so, every time he visits the shop, he has to stop and pause and reflect on the fact that this slight, jovial man with the crisp, dry commentator's voice was once the captain of Australia. That this slight, jovial man with the writer's way about him has actually faced the great Lindwall, and the Englishman Trueman, whom you might call Fred, or Freddie, depending on Trueman, and depending on the day. And not only faced them, but gently clipped them all around the paddock, as they say on the radio, which always amuses Michael because he plays on paddocks. Indeed, there are times when it crosses Michael's mind that if he didn't know, and if he were asked to pick from the customers and staff who the one-time Australian captain was, he would not give the slight, jovial Hassett a second thought. The same Hassett whose favourite line of inquiry is 'Are you right there, boys?' whenever anybody lingers long over the autographed bats.

Then his voice is nearer and it occurs to Michael for the first time since entering the shop that he might actually speak to him. Michael does not want to be spoken to, he does not even want to be observed, and so he slips away to a corner of the shop and waits for Hassett to go back to the counter where he will resume his conversation with a man his own age about a game they both played many years before — yet which they both clearly recall in all its detail. Detail enough for stories and laughter. It is only then, when the quiet, inquiring voice of Hassett has returned to the front of the shop, that he lifts his head and sees them. Bowlers boots.

He smells the leather of the soles, notes the shiny white leather of the uppers, catches the glint of the metal spikes. These are the boots of a bowler who plays on turf. Turf. Michael plays on sandy gravel pitches that are little more than short footpaths, or grounds that are no more than mown thistle and weed, or on concrete pitches covered in matting. He has never played on turf, but he knows that that is where the best of cricket is played and that the bowlers who play on turf wear boots such as these. That is what the spikes are for. They dig into the ground and they give a bowler feet to bowl with, for if your feet aren't underneath you where they ought to be you can't bowl. But boots like these give a bowler feet. And with the feet come the legs — because everybody knows that you bowl with your legs. The arm rolling over, and the delivery of the ball — that is the last part of a long, complex process. Bowlers run — and they run with their legs. The great Hall runs ten miles a game. It is the running that gives you what his science teacher calls momentum. That's a good word. He likes that word. It's almost as good as speed. But not quite. Speed is his favourite word. There is no better word in the language. The very sound of it tells you what it means. And momentum too. Momentum is the messenger of speed. When a bowler has momentum you know that speed isn't far away. Momentum, velocity, speed. All good words. And it all starts with the legs. But in order to have legs you've got to have feet, and in order to have feet you've got to have boots like these. And as he stands there he can imagine what it is to bowl with these boots, can almost imagine the snug feel of his feet inside them. He can imagine what it would be like not to lose everything just as you were about to deliver it, as he does on the sandy, slippery pitches in the paddocks that he plays on. The smooth, perfect action of the great Lindwall makes sense when you look at boots like these, because he doesn't have to worry where his feet are. Not on turf. And not in boots like these.

He has seen turf once. Seen the entrancing green and the sparkling white lines of turf. Seen the white picket fences and the deep green clubrooms of a ground where they play cricket as it is played in books. But only once. Michael bowls in tennis shoes. Everybody does. And as Michael stands before these boots, contemplating the difference between boots and tennis shoes, he becomes increasingly aware that there is an entirely other world of cricket out there, just waiting to be played. The shop always brings this world a little closer. In this shop he sees leather cricket balls, cream shirts and sleeveless sweaters. But it is to the boots that he returns because it is the boots that give you feet, and without that, everything else — the shirts, sweaters and trousers — are mere decoration.

Throughout the time he has been standing in front of the boots, Michael has been aware of the radio playing softly in the background. It is the First Test and the final day of the game, but by the early afternoon it is clear that the situation is hopeless. The great Hall is bowling with speed and laughter. Then the radio tells him that Hall stops bowling and Michael loses interest. As he leaves the shop he eyes the boots one last time.

On the train he watches the late-afternoon sun pour itself into the corners of the North Melbourne rail yards and remembers walking across the soot-blackened footbridge with his father to the workshops one morning, although he has long forgotten the reason for his being there at all. He watches the same sun melting onto the rooftops of Kensington and Newmarket — old suburbs, old houses, squashed together in rows. He knows the stops by heart after years of taking the dusty red train to and from the city. Then he watches the same sun yet again settle onto the rooftops of Essendon and all the suburbs that follow, and soon he sees the flour mills of his suburb glowing in the distance like the medieval towers of a medieval town, and all the houses become flat and square and dull and he knows he is nearing home.

During the last part of the journey, he takes a pamphlet from his pocket. It is from the district club and was sent to all the local teams. It is asking for the best young players from each club to attend a special training session, a clinic, where they can be coached and observed. Michael has had the pamphlet for a week now and looks at it every day, studying its every detail. This is where it begins, where dreams stop being faraway things, the stuff of other people's lives, and start to enter the daily world of what you do. This is how someone begins to live a dream. They open a pamphlet one day, suddenly know what needs to be done and set about doing it. That's what they all did, the greats, they didn't wait to be showered in dreams. Dreams, he knows, can be lived because ordinary people go out there into the world and live them. These are the ones for whom dreams are simply the things you do.

He has weeks to wait before the date stated on the pamphlet. Between then and now — in this red, dusty train carriage, pamphlet in hand, watching the egg-yolk sun, orange and scarlet, melting down onto the high walls of the flour mills — he will run and bowl every day, until he is barely aware that his body is performing a function. Until he is so concentrated on the task at hand that he forgets his concentration and is no longer aware of the sounds of the world around him, when he enters another dimension of living altogether in which the passage of time and the bleating of cars and trains and people belong to another, lesser world. When there is no need to be thinking of yesterday or tomorrow, or the day before or the next year, because time will have collapsed into the single moment of delivery when his arm rolls over and it all works out.

But to do this he will need feet, and to have feet he will need the boots he saw today.

The house is empty and warm from the day's heat. And quiet, the way a house that has been vacant all day is quiet. The lounge room is clean and tidied, old magazines and newspapers neatly stacked under the coffee table. In the kitchen Michael switches the small plastic radio on and sound enters the house for the first time that afternoon. Immediately, the house is transformed. The voices on the radio are excited; raised voices on a normally quiet station. They are using words such as 'extraordinary' and 'speechless' and 'unbelievable'. And then, because they can find no other words with which to express this thing that so excites them, they repeat themselves and the words 'extraordinary', 'speechless' and 'unbelievable' burst from the radio once more and fill every corner of the house which, like Michael, is stirring to the news that something extraordinary has indeed happened.

It is then that Michael hears the word 'tie' — again and again. The commentator is repeating the word, almost with a question mark after it, for it seems to Michael that there is disbelief in his voice. In all their voices, for there seem to be many commentators and they all seem to be talking at once. And it is then that he hears another word — 'historic'. The word 'historic' is now joined with the word 'tie' and the phrase 'historic tie' is uttered. The commentators have been so stirred by the events they have witnessed that it takes them a long time to form simple phrases.

Soon they calm down and are able to speak more complex sentences. And soon, Michael is being told that this was the greatest game ever played — and it is Michael who is listening with disbelief. He is leaning over the radio in the kitchen, leaning against the bench upon which the radio sits, and slowly taking in the news that this has been the greatest game of cricket ever played — and he missed it.

He can't believe that while he wandered slowly back to the Flinders Street Station through the city, while he stopped for one of the ice-cream thick shakes for which the station is famous, while he sat on the train and watched the sun melt onto the rooftops of Kensington and Newmarket, Essendon and Ascot Vale, and while he ambled back past the flour mills and along the Old Wheat Road — that this thing, this extraordinary event was unfolding without him. He missed it. And now he is being told that, mathematically, the chances of anybody — any of 'us', says a commentator — witnessing an event such as this again are infinitely small. And all the time, as the voices of the commentators and the occasional sounds of the small crowd at the ground enter the kitchen and fill the house, Michael stays bowed over the radio.

He has no memory of leaving the kitchen but he must have because he is now standing in the backyard staring at the glow of the evening sun, at the peach, plum and lemon trees and the shimmering gold-plated leaves of the passionfruit vine on the fence. Somewhere out there, a thousand miles to the sub-tropical north on the Brisbane pitch, this thing had happened and the day has been transformed into one of those days that is remembered. One of those days about which people talk and have quite specific memories — what they were doing and when and where. Just as Michael will always recall that the events of this day took place without him.

10.
Gannon

In the evening Michael emerges from his room after having devoured all the news of this game of games, to find a short, square man standing in the kitchen. He is almost as wide as he is tall. He is wearing black golfing trousers, a dark-blue cardigan and has the tanned face of a regular mid-week golfer. His hands are plunged deep into his pockets and his feet (as if he is about to drive an imaginary golf ball) are planted firmly on the floor. He looks perfectly at ease in somebody else's house. He puts his glass down on the circular table as if the kitchen were his. And when he turns to Michael, his wide, meaty hand, with its short square fingers extended towards him, it is as if he is welcoming the boy into his own home. Michael shakes the hand of this short, square man and the strength is unmistakable. His hand is hard, metallic, like the machines in Webster's factory.

Michael wants to return to his room but his father insists he stays, that he sit and drink and talk with the old man and his mate, Gannon. Michael notes again how quickly someone his father meets at the club bar becomes a mate. The boy wavers, his father repeats his invitation. Normally, he would shrug his father's drunken insistence off and go to his room anyway, but there is a guest in the house and he feels compelled to stay. And it is then that their guest, once again giving every impression of inviting the boy into his own house, points to a spare place at the table and Michael sinks onto the new, green vinyl chair.

The kitchen clock tells Michael that it is nine-thirty. It is still warm. His father and his guest have been at the golf course all afternoon and at the golf-course bar all evening. His mother is away overnight in the country as she sometimes is. Not that Michael cares about these nights now. He doesn't have to wake in the dark any more, sit by his father's bedside and explain to him what day it is, what roster he is on or who his fireman is. Not now. But his father, during these times when Rita is absent, makes a point of being the first to rise the next morning. Partly to prove to himself that he still can — and could if required to — and partly to reassure both himself and the household that he wasn't really that drunk the night before.

Their faces are sweaty from the afternoon sun and the evening's drinking, and the beer they have drunk continually pops out in beads of perspiration on their foreheads. Their guest is an ex-policeman. A detective. Michael's father and this man have been drinking all evening and when the golf-course bar closed his father invited the man home, as he always does because he never knows when the night is over. The man, this Gannon, asks Michael a few preliminary questions and Michael asks about being a detective because he has never met one before. All the time his father, with the faraway stare of the drunk, looks on with the kind of smile that readily converts to a sneer.

'You see all sorts of things that most people don't,' their guest says. 'Meet all types.' He nods, and he clearly doesn't mean the types that the likes of Michael would care to meet.

He offers an example and on one of their new, vinyl chairs he leans forward with a cold stare, and a flat, matter-of-fact tone to his voice that creates an attentive silence in the kitchen that is different from all the other silences Michael can remember. He talks, he talks. Quietly, matter-of-factly. Michael doesn't move, nor does his father, whose drunken smile has slowly drained from his face. It is possibly a minute since Gannon started talking, possibly five. His hand, which seems to have expanded in the course of the conversation, is reaching out across the table as if clutching a melon. He is illustrating a point. It is not a melon. It is, in fact, the back of a man's skull. One of those types whom the boy would not have met and would do well not to meet. One of those types he has had memorable dealings with in his past life as a detective. In front of them this Gannon then paints a vivid picture of a brick wall, made from the sort of rough, grey bricks that have recently become quite fashionable, and which, in fact, Gannon confesses he contemplated using for his own house. Michael knows the kind of bricks he is referring to and as he watches their guest's hand he feels those bricks pressed up against his own forehead, nose, cheeks, mouth and chin. The whole of his face is suddenly pressed into those bricks and he knows what comes next. He is, therefore, not surprised when Gannon's hand begins its slow descent, and that imaginary face pressed deep into that imaginary brick wall descends, unresisting, with Gannon's hand.

'I was talking to him the whole time, you understand,' he adds, in that flat, matter-of-fact voice he would no doubt have used at the time. 'And when I'd finished my little talk and we'd run out of bricks and words, I'd left half his face back there on the wall.'

He pauses for a moment and lets it all sink in.

'We couldn't touch him, you see. But we knew he was our man and the point had to be made. You understand?'

Their guest is now staring intently at Michael, waiting for a response, and Michael nods. But this man, this Gannon, keeps staring at the boy, not fully convinced by, or satisfied with, the nod he has received.

Ten minutes before, Gannon had the vague eyes of the drunk. Now he doesn't. He has been sobered by the tale. Sobered by violence. And Michael knows that this man is as at home with violence as he is with other people's kitchens. Gannon sits back for a moment, pours himself a drink and savours it as if it were the first of the evening.

A silence follows as he drinks, and Michael's father covers that particular kind of silence that people such as Gannon bring with them with a description of Gannon's house.

He's no longer a detective — he doesn't say what he does now — but he lives on two acres of land to the north of the suburb; a new double-storey house in which he lives with his wife, his beautiful daughter, and his swimming pool. And even as he listens, Michael is idly wondering how an ex-detective manages to come by a mansion with a swimming pool. He does not know much about wages or salaries, but he does suspect that policemen don't live in mansions as a rule.

Gannon then extends an invitation to Vic and Michael that they visit his house, swim in his pool, and meet his wife and daughter.

'But don't get any ideas, young man,' he adds.

At first Michael doesn't understand, then he realises that Gannon is referring to his beautiful daughter and Michael quickly assures him that he hasn't got any ideas. He says so in the same matter-of-fact tone that Gannon uses, so that he won't get the wrong idea. Michael has been learning about irony at school. His teacher calls it a weapon. But Michael can tell that Gannon has no time for such weaponry. He can tell that in the eyes of the Gannons of this world, irony is for the weak. And so when Michael says that he hasn't got any ideas he says so in a way that ensures there can be no misunderstandings and that he doesn't come out sounding smart. Gannon lives in the simplified world of violence, he brings its basic laws with him wherever he goes, and he doesn't expect them to be contradicted.

He tells Michael his daughter's name. Does Michael know her?

'No', says Michael. 'I don't know her. I've never met her.'

'But you will,' Gannon continues. 'When you

visit. Won't he, Vic?' He turns to Vic as if having completely forgotten that his host was there.

They then fall into a discussion of the man's daughter, his house and his swimming pool. All the time his father's face wears a look that Michael has seen all too often before and which he can only describe as idiotic. A look of idiot admiration covers his face, already glowing from too much beer and too much sun. And, not for the first time, Michael is ashamed of the idiot grin on his father's face. His father, he knows, is not an idiot. His father has a way with words and a subtlety of thinking that the Gannons of this world will always sniff at with distrust. Yet his father is nodding admiringly and approvingly at the stories, the house and the beautiful daughter that all belong to their guest, this man, Gannon, who is a short, square animal. Whom Michael has never met before and hopes never to meet again — who makes Bruchner, their neighbour, look like a sook.

Once, at times like these, his father might have been drinking with his work mates and they would discuss their work — steam, diesel, engines and the art of driving. Now he brings the likes of Gannon into the house.

When their guest rises to leave — as perfectly at ease in the hallway as he was in the kitchen — he extends his hand to the boy and Michael feels once more its crushing strength, like the metal hammers in Webster's factory that press scrap into spare engine parts or ashtrays.

The first thing that comes back to Vic when he wakes in the middle of the night is the look on Michael's face that evening when he slobbered his silly drunken words to an indifferent Gannon. They observe each other frequently now, more than they have in the past, and Vic is increasingly aware of the disapproval in his son's eyes.

But it is not the disapproval in his son's eyes that is occupying his thoughts at this mad hour when no one ought to be thinking. It is something else quite different. What is occupying Vic's mind, what he is dwelling on in the darkness, is the confidence the boy exudes more and more lately. The confidence he displays — when he isn't looking, that is, with disapproval upon his poor old dad — is something that makes him almost untouchable, and Vic is wondering where on earth he got it from. There is a sense of great expectations in those sixteen-year-old eyes that Vic never had at that age or any other. Or, if he ever did, the years wiped it away, and he has since forgotten. The boy has his dream. Michael never speaks of it, but he doesn't have to. And Vic is happy for him, even if he wishes it was golf, not cricket — about which he knows little. Vic gave Michael his old set of clubs and taught him how to play whenever the boy would let him. The boy knows his mind, always has. And it was never going to be golf that he took up in the end, but this cricket, which Vic never played and which is a mystery to him. Not an interesting mystery; the mystery to Vic about the game is why anybody bothers with it. But the boy does. It's where his dream lies. He's got the certain concentrated look of someone confident of living it. And he just might, thinks Vic. He just might.

Maybe that's the way it works. Each generation gets better, moves further away from all the faults, the petty flaws, the traps and the sheer bulldust that shagged their parents' chances of ever living up to their dreams. That, and all the odds that seemed to be constantly stacked up against you. The buggers who were born into their dreams and treated dreams as if they owned them all, and made it plain that only a precious few got to live them because there were only so many dreams to go around. Perhaps each generation gets better. Gets smarter, gets something that the poor buggers who went before didn't have. That something extra that doesn't take shit for an answer and doesn't cop, for a moment, all the bulldust that there are only so many dreams to go around and they've all been sold at birth anyway. Maybe, just maybe, it all rises and falls, like good times and bad. And perhaps, in time, from time to time, a generation comes along that gets what it wants. Perhaps Michael's is that generation. The one that all the work was for, the one that it was all about — the shame, the slog and the being shagged over time and again by smart bastards. Perhaps the look of great expectation in Michael's eyes was always going to be at the end of it all. Even if to everyone along the line, who had to work their lives away in order to bring that look into existence, it was never apparent. But perhaps it was the thing that dragged them all, the generations that went before, from day to day anyway, even if they didn't know it. The generations were refining themselves, smoothing out their rough edges, slowly casting off the look of the born loser for the confident eyes that spoke of great expectations. That very look Michael now wears more often than not.

Yes, Vic rolls over in bed as the thought rolls through his head, perhaps Michael's look is the point of it all, and always was. Perhaps his is that generation that comes along every so often and gets what it wants: and he's the one, out of all of them, the whole family history, the lucky bastard who's going to live his dream. And good luck to him if he does. But as soon as Vic thinks this, as soon as he finds himself quietly smiling at the prospect of it all, he's suddenly thinking of engines and diesels and dreams, and the way things always turn out lousy in the end, the way they did for him. In this world of theirs that will, of course, never change. And, just as suddenly, all that contagious confidence in the sixteen-year-old eyes of his son evaporates, and his whole being is heavy with all the old doubts that dragged his lot down, those who start out with dreams of a kind, not big dreams, not grand dreams, but dreams enough to occupy a mind of modest ambition, and wind up with the likes of Gannon in the house.

II.

Webster is Restless

In another part of the suburb, Webster is restless. He roams about the many rooms of his house, from the dining room to the billiards room, the lounge room and the library, but never stays any more than a few minutes in any one of them. His house has many rooms but in none of these rooms does he feel at ease. All of these rooms, the library, the games room, the sitting room, were intended — and Webster chose the house for its many rooms, so he has no one to blame — to put him at ease. To relax him, to allow him to indulge himself in the many interests he assumed he would cultivate in his mature years. Webster is fifty-eight years old and although his hair is grey at the sides, it is still thick and wavy, a good head of hair, the head of a man with considerable life left in him — and at this stage of life he ought to be indulging himself in those little interests which he always promised himself he would eventually cultivate.

Webster has four factories. The last of these being the one he built at the intersection of the two main streets of the suburb. They all crush or cut metal into parts that are useful to other factories, who eventually press them and screw them and bolt them into objects that are useful to people. That is the stuff of his life. Some of these objects — a lawnmower, a washing machine, wheelbarrow — find their way into his house and back into his life. It's not something he takes any particular pride in or interest in. They are just objects, and they work or they fall apart as these things do. But this is his gift. He is good at providing the parts that combine with other parts and become indispensable domestic objects. He has never had to work particularly hard at it. He has four factories and he employs hundreds of people. And although he could have lived anywhere, he chose to live in this suburb because he liked the wide look of the land. And there was no shortage of wide rambling mansions left over from the previous century when the suburb was a farming community. Here he could have the mansion and the sprawling grounds that he'd always sought, and which he found not far from the factory site itself.

He bought it all just after the war. The mansion and the grazing land that surrounded it belonged to the descendents of an old pioneering family, a family that had once possessed wealth and power. They weren't happy about selling up, but in the end Webster persuaded them with the sheer weight of his money, and the mansion and the sprawling grounds that surrounded it became his. He should have been happy. Or, if not happy, then at least content.

But tonight, like so many nights, Webster is restless, and he roams through the many rooms of his rambling house, never lingering any more than a few moments in any one of them. His wife is reading in their bedroom, a wide, spacious room that looks down over the gardens. The cook-cum-maid is cleaning up after dinner before withdrawing to her room at the back of the kitchen. He is happy with his wife and has never sought the company of other women. It is, he knows, a good marriage — and he knows he can expect no better. There are no children in the house but he has long since accustomed himself to this and feels no sense of loss or sadness. It is not, in fact, something that he thinks of all that often. The cause of his restlessness that won't let him linger in any one room is not to be found in this or anything like it, in any of these mere personal matters. Nor is he bored, like those characters in the plays that his wife drags him to. Those continental types who mope about the stage complaining that their lives are boring, and so on and so forth (as the smarter characters say in these plays that call themselves 'slices of life'). No, it is none of that either for he knows he can expect no better life than the one he is living. It is, quite simply, the unrelenting, irrefutable sense of the utter uselessness of it all. His life, that is. And the objects that he makes. These objects that are useful to people and utterly meaningless to him. He can't remember when it first came upon him, this feeling, but he can't remember not having it. He is doing, he knows, what he is best at and he can't imagine doing anything else. But this sense that it is all utterly useless — no matter how well he might do it — came out of nowhere one day and settled upon him (possibly just after he moved into his house), and it hasn't gone away. It is there, in greater or lesser degrees, every day. And on nights such as these it leaves him, not sad, depressed, anxious or bored, but restless.

Webster tells his wife that tonight he will work late. He tells her he will sleep in one of the rooms set aside for guests so as not to disturb her in the night. She smiles and nods and thinks nothing of it for it is the custom of Webster to sleep in the guest room on such occasions. It is, she tells him, unnecessary, as she is a deep sleeper. He won't disturb her. Webster knows it takes a lot to disturb his wife's sleep but he takes his pyjamas to the spare room all the same.

The house sinks into silence. Mrs Webster lays the book she is reading down beside her on the bedside table, switches the lamp off, and the house sinks into darkness. Soon after, Mrs Webster sinks into a deep sleep. Everything sinks: the last image that passes through her mind being that of her husband hunched over his desk in his study below, silently labouring through the night, submerged in work.

There is a full moon and a silvery film falls across the garden. Webster follows the winding, gravel path down to a shed in a corner of the grounds, a considerable distance from the house. The most relaxed he has been all evening, Webster strolls through his gardens — which are as big as a modest public park — as if it were the middle of the afternoon. A small army of gardeners created these gardens out of the farming paddocks they once were. Where cows once roamed, Webster now strolls. A team of gardeners works through the days and weeks of the year, mowing the lawns, caring for the shrubs and trees, the out-houses, the gardener's sheds, and occasionally dredging the small lake in one of the corners of the property.

The grounds of Webster's house may be as large as a modest public park, but he always strolls through them with absolute confidence and assurance. And when he stands long enough in one spot to take them in, he stands with the same proprietorial certainty that he does whenever on one of the four floors of his four factories. The gates of his driveway are always open, anybody can enter at any time — for whatever reason — and sometimes do. But this is Webster's property, nothing can touch him here, and he is at his most relaxed when strolling through its gardens — day or night.

At the shed he unlocks the doors and opens them up to the light of the full moon. And the instant he does a silver light falls across a canvas tarpaulin. He slowly pulls the canvas back and the gleaming white chrome and black enamel of a long, low, sleek sports car become visible. He stands for a moment admiring the lines of the thing, then folds the tarpaulin and drops it on the ground beside the car. He has the only key to the shed and no one except for his chauffeur — who regularly cleans and tunes the motor — knows what is in there. He has never told his wife. It is his one, secret indulgence. His one infidelity in an otherwise faithful marriage. And if she has ever wondered what is inside this locked, uninspiring gardener's shed in a far-flung corner of the gardens, she has never said so. Either because she doesn't particularly care about the contents of a remote gardener's shed, or because she senses that this is his one secret indulgence, his one trifling infidelity in an otherwise faithful marriage — and chooses to keep it that way.

It is a still, warm night and he winds the driver's side window down, and quietly taps his fingers on the leather-covered steering wheel before turning the ignition key. It is possibly the one moment he prizes over all the other moments to follow, when his hand, the slightest of tremors just visible, reaches out for the key to bring the beast to life. After savouring his moment he turns the key and the rumble is instantaneous. But straightaway the engine settles to a hum. The car is as still as the night, the engine barely appears to be on at all.

Slowly, so as not to disturb the night too soon, he eases out of the shed and quietly follows the winding gravel pathway out into the suburb, noting as he does that nothing in the house has stirred. Its many rooms are dark, the moonlight falls across the slate roof like moonlight from a dream, and the lights at the front of the house illuminate the steps leading up to the front door as they will throughout the night.

12

An Ambulance Arrives

A silly thing to do, to go falling over like that. How many times have I crossed that street? You wouldn't think you could fall over just crossing a street, but there it is. I wasn't watching where I was going, I don't remember what I was thinking. I just remember catching my foot and thinking that that was lucky, I could have fallen over, and then I did Suddenly I was face down in the dirt. I let my basket go, with my purse and my keys, and it was upside down in front of me. It was the sight of my things all spilt out on the road that bothered me most at first. Well, I thought, can't lie around here all day, old girl. You tripped, you fell. A silly thing to do. Just silly, that's all. Hardly important. Time to get up, brush yourself down and pick up that basket.

You fall down, you get up. You've done it before, you can do it again. It's been happening all your life. That's what I told myself. But I couldn't. And that was when I felt it. This pain. I don't remember feeling it when I was lying there. But as soon as I moved, as soon as I said, c'mon old girl, lift yourself, as soon as I naturally went to do what comes next, I felt it. It nearly took my breath away, and on stinking hot days like these I don't have too much breath to give away. You can be old, and still be thinking young. It's a trap. I wasn't watching, I wasn't thinking. I fell. And as much as I said, c'mon old girl, lift yourself, I couldn't. Every time I tried, this pain stopped me. It was all I could do to just roll on my side, look around the street, the town, and wave someone over. I'm sorry, I'm sorry, I kept on saying to Gus the greengrocer. I think I've broken something, Gus, I can't move. I'm sorry. He kept saying it's all right, Mrs C, it's all right. It's good of him to call me that because I'm not a Mrs, am I? There's no ring on my marriage finger, and there never has been. But he's met Vic. From those days when Vic and Rita were living in the next town — a railway town — and would ride their bicycles down every Sunday to see me. We'd go for a slow walk through the town on the warm days, and when we met someone we'd stop and I'd say, 'This is my son.' I couldn't help it. It'd just burst out of me whenever we met someone. That's how it was with Gus, the first time I introduced Vic. He was loading his van with crates of vegetables and we stopped and I said good afternoon, Gus, this is my boy, all six foot of him. I must have stared too long at Vic then because he said that's enough, Ma, he always calls me Ma. I embarrass him a lot you see, in public. I don't mean to. It just bursts out of me, all this talk. From then on, whenever I went to Gus's for the greens — which was every other day — he called me Mrs C. He didn't have to because he could see there was nothing on my finger. But he called me Mrs C from then on. So, there I was lying face down on the road with my basket upside down beside me, saying, 'I'm sorry, I'm sorry, Gus.' And Gus was saying, 'It's all right, Mrs C.' But I knew it wasn't. He couldn't move me without hurting me. That was when he called for his helper and they both carried me into his shop.

Now I'm sitting in the back of this thing, I'm saying farewell to the town, I've got the key to the front door of my little house, and I'm wondering if I'm ever going to use it again. You see these things go past in the street, roaring off with their bells ringing, and you think, 'Oh God, some poor coot's in there.' Then you don't think any more of it. And by the time you get to the shops or the bank, or whatever it is that you've set out to do that day, the poor coot that's inside could be dead. It happens. Every day. Ambulances come and go. But you've stopped thinking about it, and just as well. It's no good going about your business thinking things like that.

Then, one day, you find yourself inside one of these things, looking out. It's a different view. Not one I'm all that happy about having. But, well, I'm seventy-seven, and at least I'm still looking at something. At least those bloody bells aren't ringing. At least we're not speeding. In fact, once you get used to it, it's almost pleasant lying back here and watching the countryside go by. The driver and his assistant call out occasionally, but most of the time they just chat away without me, mostly about the cricket yesterday. Everybody is talking about that game of cricket yesterday: the driver, the radio, even Gus the greengrocer — who doesn't much care for the game — was talking about it while we waited in his shop for this limousine of a thing to arrive. I don't feel the bumps, which is just as well, 'cause this hip's giving me hell; and my throat's not much better. Summer colds, they're always the worst. And all the barley sugar and lemon juice in the world doesn't seem to help. Only beer. A glass of ice-cold beer does the trick every time. For a while. In fact, I wouldn't mind one now. Not that there's any beer to be had around here. They've got everything else, mind you.

At this pace, and we're going nice and slow, we won't get to Vic's till evening. He'll have something cool in the fridge for this throat. Summer colds. I always get them, and they're always the worst. I don't know why I couldn't have just stayed where I was. But he insisted, this young bloke, a nice bloke — he insisted I have some family around me till the hip gets better. And I said the only family I've got is Vic. That's my son. My sisters, Katherine, Frances — they're gone. Agnes, well, she's in Adelaide. She's a nun, I said. And they nodded. Agnes, I said. She got the beautiful name, she got all the looks that the rest of us never much had — and she gave it all to God. Which leaves Vic. They all nodded to each other again. The next thing I know I'm sitting up in this thing enjoying a slow, quiet ride to town. On the inside looking out. It's not a view I'm happy to have and I'll be glad to see Vic. I'll be glad to see anybody. I'll be glad to just get out and be part of the world again, rather than lying back here and looking at it go by. I've never been one for watching things go by, and I don't like the feeling. The feeling that if I let it keep going by for too long it just might not come back. The sun's dribbling into the hills over there like the yolk of a big, country egg. I always loved sunsets, when I was young. I loved a good sunset. But they make me uneasy now. It'll be dark soon, and I don't like the idea of arriving in the dark.

There's something wrong about arriving in the dark. Shifty types arrive in the dark. Kings that aren't kings any more arrive in the dark. Strangers arrive in the dark. But not me. So I wish they'd just get the whole thing over and done with and speed up a bit.

13.

Two Photographs

There is only one sound that matters. Speed. It is the day after Gannon's visit and the house has been cleaned so that no sign of his presence is left. And as the ambulance containing Vic's mother moves slowly and steadily towards the suburb, slowly and steadily so as to avoid the bumps, Michael throws a ball down the yard and hears it smack against the back fence. There are still times in summer when he takes to the yard and resumes his destruction of the back fence. Behind him the house is lit up, open to the night. Tension is always there, like it was tonight. You don't think it's there and someone tries to do a simple thing like take a photograph and it all comes out. You wonder where it comes from because it comes so fast. But there's no point asking. It's just there — the rattle of a dish, the closing of a door, the sudden thud of a book landing on the newly carpeted lounge-room floor — it's always ready to strike. That's why it comes so fast. Radio and television fill the house with talk and music, but when the tension is bad neither the television nor the radio help.

Yes, it's always there and it takes very little to make the tension speak, like it did tonight when Rita tried to do a simple thing and take a photograph of everyone. The family. Rita has a new camera. She is not someone who goes in for gadgets — not that a camera is a gadget. But this camera — which she recently bought in the country on one of her trips demonstrating washing machines and new electric fry pans to stores full of country housewives — comes with a device. Two, in fact. It develops its own photographs and you can look at the photos minutes after having taken the shot. The photographs are not good quality, not the same as the photographs that come back from the chemist in the Old Wheat Road. But it's fun to look at them straight away. Or it should be. The other little trick this camera has is the switch next to the shutter release button. This is the time delay, and when activated it allows the person taking the photograph to be in the photograph.

It is a game. And tonight it was meant to be a game. A bit of light-hearted fun. A lark with the new gadget. The television was switched off. The radio silenced. Rita arranged Vic so that the armchair in which he habitually slumps after dinner was turned away from the television and towards the camera, which was propped on a kitchen stool. His right arm hung by his side, still clutching the newspaper he was reading before Rita arranged the scene. In his other hand he held his reading glasses. Tonight he is wearing a mustard-coloured pullover Rita knitted for him years before, for they are experiencing one of those odd summer evenings when the temperature suddenly drops and they are back to winter. It is a pullover he often wore to work and which still has the faint smell of steam and cinders, still has the capacity to bring the smell of the job into the house; back from the dead and into life again. Perhaps this is why he continues to wear it, in preference to other, smarter pullovers. But Vic is not one for smart pullovers. The old jumpers will do. Rita knew it would end up in the photograph and as she arranged everyone for the shot she'd wished all over again, like she often does, that she'd never knitted the damn thing. Michael had been dragged away from the cushion that he always rests his head on while reclining on the floor, and sat beside his father's armchair.

Rita instructed Vic and Michael to remain perfectly still, then rehearsed what she had to do.

Satisfied, she'd then told Vic and Michael that she was now ready to take the photograph. And as she pressed all the necessary buttons she instructed them both to smile, not realising that neither Vic nor Michael had followed her instructions. Vic's jaw was set firm and he eyed the camera with the glum expression of a man whose time was being wasted. He was still gripping his paper and glasses, impatient to resume his reading. Michael too stared blankly back at the camera as if eager to be somewhere other than in the picture. But Rita, who slipped onto her seat on the count of four, saw none of this and beamed back with the same bright-eyed smile she always kept for the camera when she was a girl.

When the shot was taken, Vic replaced his glasses and opened his paper at the article he was reading before the photograph intervened, and Michael slumped back onto the floor, resuming his study of the sports pages. Rita had lingered by the square hole in the wall — the servery that connects the kitchen with the lounge room — and, still smiling, had jigged slightly from one foot to the other while the photograph was developing. She heard the crisp newsprint of Vic's paper as he turned the pages, noted the absent-minded *thump thump* of Michael's foot on the lounge-room floor. She'd watched the minutes tick by on the kitchen clock then peeled back a layer of thick, developing paper to reveal the photograph beneath, and the smile had fallen from her lips the instant she did. And with the smile, the expectation too drained from her face. Her hand, still holding the photograph, fell limply to her side.

'What's the bloody point,' she was suddenly muttering.

It was then that Vic had looked up over the rim of his glasses and Michael had turned from the paper. Rita glanced at the photo once again, the glum face of Vic, the moody — what is it? sneer almost — of Michael. And that silly smile of hers. Why bother? Why bloody bother at all? It was the very thing she didn't want to see — a portrait of an unhappy family, a snap of a failed marriage, and she wasn't going to have it in the house. It was then that she had drifted into the kitchen, torn the thing into strips and dumped the unhappy jigsaw in the bin. The lid of the bin snapped shut and the kitchen chair upon which she sat for the photograph was flung back to its place at the table.

'What's the bloody point?' Rita offered the room again, only louder.

Michael had then entered the kitchen and stood beside her. Yet even now, walking back to his mark in the yard, he has no memory of rising from the floor, from the sports pages, and taking the journey from lounge room to kitchen in order to be by his mother's side. But he had. And, suddenly, there he was.

'We'll do it again,' he'd said.

'Forget it.'

'No, we can do it again,' he'd repeated, looking at his father through the servery. 'Can't we?'

'Of course,' Vic nodded, out of his chair and standing on the carpet, eager to make amends.

But Rita had just shaken her head.

'Is it too much to get a smile out of you lot?'

'We can do it again. And we'll all smile. Look!'

Michael had grinned then. An idiotic grin, and the flicker of a smile returned to Rita's face and before she had time to object any further she was pressing the time delay button once more and counting the seconds before assuming her seat in the group portrait.

When she peeled the second photo back the first thing she saw was Vic's smile. It was a big smile, alight with laughter, as if the photographer had just told him a particularly amusing tale. A real smile, she could see that. She's seen all his smiles come and go and she can tell when he means it. He meant this one, all right. This was one of Vic's old grins, the kind of smile he was full of once, but the kind of smile she sees too little of now. And Michael had that idiot grin of a boy playing with the idea of laughter, playing with the whole notion of having to smile for a camera and having so much fun doing so that in the end he couldn't help but smile. So it was with Rita. Her smile was awkward, as if the whole business were just a bit too silly really, and she'd been dragged into a bit of tomfoolery that she hadn't counted on, and because of that she had this smile on her face, that — if it were a laugh — would be a titter.

Within minutes an unhappy family had been transformed into a happy family. It is precisely the kind of photograph that, in years to come, she will look back upon fondly and see only the smiles and remember only the laughter.

And why not? Why bloody well not? If that's what it takes to get on with things, she muses, then so be it. Why bloody well not? A little bit of forgetfulness here and there. It's not a bloody crime. And everybody takes two photographs, don't they? Just in case the first one doesn't work out. Even the happy families. Don't they? She poses the question to the silence of the kitchen, the photograph lying on the table, and receives only silence in reply.

There is a sudden crack, like a rifle shot, and inside the house Rita jumps as a worn cork ball, still retaining a few smudges of red paint, ricochets from the back fence to the side fence and onto the lawn. This fence, where the white stumps have been painted, has already been repaired many times, and will need to be repaired again. The whip crack of the ball hitting the fence pierces the still, summer air the way it always did, and alerts the whole neighbourhood that Michael is at it again, for nothing travels like the sound of speed on a summer's night.

In the hazy twilight the painted stumps glow at the back of the yard. Soon it will be dark, but darkness comes slowly on these nights and there is time for one more delivery, and one more after that. The sound of the ball hitting the fence pierces the still, summer air and seems to be everywhere. He has already trained today but the tension has driven him out into the yard and he is convinced that he hasn't bowled so fast all day. That he is bowling at his fastest when he should be exhausted, and he is becoming gradually convinced that he has never bowled so fast in his life.

As he bowls, the twilight settling into darkness, he is learning a few things about tension. If it can do this, maybe it isn't all bad. He is beginning to learn that you can use it; that it can be the difference between being fast and not being fast. Not all houses have this thing, this tension, and maybe he will one day learn to be grateful that his does. Tension, like speed, just might be a gift too. And if you receive the gift of tension, you should learn to use it, and nurture it, because in the end it will give you speed. Perhaps enough to give you that little bit extra that turns heads.

It is then that the flyscreen door opens, and he turns to see his mother standing in the doorway.

'That's it,' she calls. 'Enough! I don't want to hear that sound again tonight.'

She slams the door shut and returns to whatever room in the house she came from. He tosses the ball into the bucket by the shed. It is dark now, the stumps, fence and fruit trees in the yard are all in shadow, and he is suddenly exhausted.

The next morning there is pain in his back. Just a nagging thing. Everybody bowls with pain. The great Lindwall did. Behind all the poetry of the perfect action was pain — and tiredness. And just as no one saw the tiredness, no one would have seen the pain that must surely have been there after a lifetime of speed.

The best will be at the district training session. Not just from his suburb, but all the suburbs around them. If he is going to bowl with the kind of speed that turns heads, he will need to summon up everything he has. And the pain will simply become something that everyone has. Something to be carried and forgotten and not remarked upon because it is unremarkable.

He has bowled at the local school throughout the spring and summer, and every step he has taken is now recorded on the ground. Every step he has taken has left a worn patch in the dried field, and the history of his summer is written in the grass.

14.

Hay Ride

What was a swaying field of ripe wheat until a few days before, is now flat paddock. The faded red harvester, its job done, sits motionless in the distance beside the farmhouse. Rectangular hay bales dot the landscape and the still evening air is drenched with the sweet smell of recently cut hay. The field is dry, the smell is a damp one. The ground they are walking on has been flattened by machines and feet, but the stubble is still springy. Leftover straw is strewn all about them.

Kathleen Marsden is carrying a dinner the sisters of the Home have prepared for her — sandwiches in a brown paper bag and a banana. She holds the bag like someone who doesn't quite know what to do with it, as if she would gladly throw it away if only there were somewhere to throw it, but there is only the wide open field beaten flat by machines and feet. The old cart that has just dropped them off is rolling slowly and a little uncertainly back to the farmhouse, the tractor that pulls it weaving in and out of the hay bales.

It is the last Friday of the year, the day before New Year's Eve. Summer heat is upon them and the evening is still light and warm. The church for which Michael plays cricket has organised the event. The small tractor labours back and forth, from the farmhouse to the open field, gradually dropping the party in small groups where a long table stands, already cluttered with church food.

The farm is north of the suburb. The city has not yet reached it, but it has the look of a place that is about to disappear and pass into local history. The rusted machinery by the distant wire fence is clearly from another time; as are the rhythms of the farm itself. Although the work is completed for the moment, the rhythms of the farm are imprinted on the place: in the slow, weaving motion of the tractor, the leisurely breeze, and the drawl of the farmer when he greeted the party of visitors at his gate. The city may not have reached the farm yet, but the frontier of the suburbs is ever moving and moving closer with every day. Michael and Kathleen Marsden stroll past the table, ignoring it. Like an arrow that has already been fired, the city is heading towards them, and it is not difficult for Michael to imagine streets and salubriously named avenues being carved out of the open field upon which they are now standing.

There is a pond near the wire fence, close to the road they came along in their procession of church cars. Trees too dark to name rise from its banks, and when Kathleen Marsden stops briefly and asks where they are going Michael stares at the pond and nods in its direction. It is still early in the evening, but already — even from the distance at which they stand — Michael can see the occasional flash of white shirts and bright tops, hear laughter as clear as church bells, and spot the flare of struck matches and the tips of cigarettes, blinking their signals of invitation out across the open field. Michael can see and read these signals, so too can Kathleen Marsden. This is why she has stopped.

Again she asks where they are walking to and again he simply nods in the direction of the pond. But this time she asks 'why?' and he has no answer. She has no desire to cross the field to the pond where the others are smoking cigarettes and laughing in the dark, and neither does Michael, but he feels that they ought to be going there. Even from where they stand he can recognise some of that distant laughter, and just as he has no love of the team or the crowd, he has no desire to troop off in a gang and join that group by the pond whose distant laughter he knows and doesn't like. As they stand there, both recognising that neither of them really wants to go to those shady trees near the pond, Michael looks down at the right hand of Kathleen Marsden, clutching the brown paper bag containing her sandwiches and the freckled banana. He imagines those sandwiches being prepared and carefully cut by the sisters of the Home, he imagines Kathleen Marsden taking them, and saying thank you, but not wanting them, and he imagines her plotting to ditch that brown paper bag and freckled banana at the first opportunity. But no opportunity came along and now after being collected from the Home in the same car in which Michael was driven, she is still bearing her burden.

A small transistor radio breaks into song from the shadowy banks of the pond and spreads through the quiet evening air. It is a familiar, silly song and they both turn their heads back towards the source of this disturbance. 'Tedious' is the word that floats across Michael's mind as he listens to the familiar lyrics of this popular summer song. Tedious. The word is not new to him because Michael is a reader. But it is not a word he would use among his school friends. The word 'tedious' would stir the schoolyard in the same way that his mother's dresses stir the street. It is a word that needs to be shared with the right friend. And Kathleen Marsden is just the one to share this observation with; but not just yet. Not while she's still Kathleen Marsden. Not until she becomes Kate — as she is known to her friends. And it is while he is slowly shaking his head from side to side, while that tiny transistor radio continues to fill the entire arc of the horizon with its silliness, and while he is imagining a point at which Kathleen Marsden just might become Kate, that her lips slowly open and a single word drops quietly from them, while she too shakes her head slowly from side to side.

'Tedious.'

The music stops, it is now dark and the smile on Kathleen Marsden's lips is in shadow. But it's there, all right. As they turn back towards the tractor, the cart and a fresh party of church guests, it seems for all the world to Michael that here is a girl who can read his thoughts. The other possibility is that his thoughts were easy enough to read and the word she had uttered in response to the music had been clearly written in his eyes all along. That, or quite simply, Kathleen Marsden had the same response to the song and used the same word to describe it. He prefers the first. He likes the idea of this girl knowing his thoughts before he speaks them.

Near the table they quietly watch everybody. They are removed from the comings and goings of the occasion, but somehow, without moving or speaking, seem to be part of it. The brown paper bag is on her lap. They're not there yet, he thinks. Not yet. Kate would just eat the sandwiches without a second thought; Kathleen doesn't know what to do with them.

Then, as if the hours were minutes, a car door is slamming in the warm suburban night as the sweet smell of watered lawns rises to meet him. He is standing on the footpath and Kathleen Marsden is walking quickly back along the front path of the Home. A voice is calling from the front seat of the car asking Michael if he is fine to get back home and he turns to say he is. Yes, yes, he is quite sure. And as the car drives out from the kerb into that sweet suburban night, he turns back to the Home, just in time to see a wedge of yellow light fan the doorway, and Kathleen Marsden disappear.

He stands on the footpath, longer than is necessary, gazing once more upon the mystery of the place. Only now it is a different kind of mystery. A small part of St Catherine's Girls' Home is now familiar and far from lessening the mystery of the place it enriches it. The mystery of the place is growing. Once it was the old building itself with its windows and doors and cast-iron patterns that made him stop in the street and stare. Now he has seen that mighty door at the front of the Home open and close, and a small part of the mystery it contains has come into his life. It is like entering a story, or strolling up the canvas path of a painting. Even though he is not permitted past the front driveway, he is entering the house nonetheless.

On the way back, all along that short walk that leads from the Home to his street, the sweet scent of watered gardens and lawns rises to meet him. In those few hours he was away, when he was driven to the hayride, when he walked towards the pond, and when he was driven back to the Home, they were out — all of them. The gardeners of the suburb. They were out watering their lawns and gardens and filling the air with the scent of cut grass, damp concrete, flowers, gravel and wet bitumen, which is the rich, dense scent of a suburb and a suburb alone.

15.

Father Unknown

I've had it, Ivy, I said. I'm sick with it. I'm sick with the worry. And you can get an idea of the state I was in, because I didn't know her all that well, and I didn't know what she was going to say, or even what she thought of me. Or if it was going to ruin everything, or if the whole ceremony would be called off there and then. I just knew I had to say it and say it fast. Get it off my back. So with my best hat in my hands — darned before I left — and my heart in my mouth, I said I've had it, Ivy. I'm sick with it, the moment I sat down in one of those soft, cool armchairs she kept for visitors. And she gives me a comforting tap on the knee because she's seen a few things, Ivy. She knew how to settle you down, that was her gift, she could calm anybody down and get them to talk like they've never talked to anyone before, drunks and no-hopers, that was what she did and the Prahran police looked after her for it. She had the gift of saying the right thing at the right time, just like she did to me that Sunday. And so she taps me on the knee and says what is it, with Rita in the other room all the time wondering what on earth we were up to.

I just let it out there and then, because I had to. It's the licence, I say. And I leave it at that for the moment, and she's staring at me because she hasn't the foggiest what I'm talking about. The certificate, Ivy. They'll need the father's and mother's names and particulars. You can have mine any time, that's not a problem, but you can't have the father's. Oh, I can give you his name if you like, but it won't mean a thing because Vic never knew him, and I suppose you could say the same for me — except for a few months, if you know what I mean, Ivy. She's staring at me all the time, this good woman, she nods and smiles, and all the time she's nodding and smiling at me I'm sick inside. Because I feel like I've brought it with me, this stain. This awful stain. And it's making me sick that something that happened so long ago, so far away still has the power to do all this. Not because I care, not much. They can say all they like about me and already have, all those years ago. But Vic, what did he do? What did he ever do, but get born? And now we're going to have to write something down on that certificate, Ivy, and I don't know what it can be. I don't know what it is we can find to say. Then the priest, and I don't know what to tell him either. I'm sick with it, Ivy. I'm sick with the worry of it all being a disaster, a disaster that's all my fault because I've got this thing, this stain. And it just keeps spreading. I wouldn't mind if only it'd just stop with me, but it doesn't. Do I make myself plain, Ivy? She nods and smiles again, and I know she understands exactly what I mean. I don't tell her this — not that she's all that religious, because she doesn't appear to be, but because she's so practical, this little woman — so I don't tell her that maybe if I weren't around any more the stain would stop with me. And it wouldn't hurt anybody else, and there wouldn't be any disasters, disasters that I know would be all my doing. I'd stay away, I'd go away forever, never see my boy again if I knew that would give him a clean start and make him happy, because that would make me happy. But it doesn't work like that. Does it?

While I'm thinking all this, keeping this bit to myself, she leans forward and taps me on the knee again and says don't worry about the priest. Leave the priest to me, and she nods, this good, sensible woman, and I know that that bit at least is all right. She knows the priest, the priest is one of hers. Not a word will be mentioned. Nobody's going to say a word, she says, because I won't have it. She gives me a firm nod, this little woman, and there's a don't-mix-with-me look in those eyes all of a sudden. And I know it's not for me, it's just to let me know that this is the look that she'll be keeping for anybody who might dream of opening their mouths or even so much as breathe a word. It's to let me know that she's got this look in her and that she knows just when to use it. And that when she does, nobody mixes with her.

Then she points to the table beside us, and for the first time since stepping into the house — and it's a large, open house, big enough to have a guests' room, which we're sitting in — I notice that there's a silver teapot on the table with some scones and jam that look like they've just been done. As she picks up a cup and a saucer, she quietly says, and as for the certificate, Mrs C, don't you give it a thought. And she lets the milk settle in the cup before stirring it in. It'll just say 'Father Unknown'. But nobody will see that bit that doesn't need to know. She gives me that look again that assures me nobody will know that doesn't need to know because she won't have it.

We talk about the china, because you don't see the kind of china she serves up all that often, and the house and the many rooms and her daughters. My ghosts have gone for now. I can feel they've gone, and I'm happy to talk about the little things. I'm listening to this good woman talk about her house and her china, and just as I'm thinking how lucky she is to be living without ghosts she says it. You're not so alone, she says, staring out the window. I'm not so sure what she means, and I say I'm not. I've got my boy, even if he's not such a boy any more, and I've got my sisters, even if I don't see them. I know they're there. She shakes her head. In your troubles, I mean, Mrs C — and it's good of her to call me that because she knows I'm not. I don't say anything because I'm not sure I'm meant to. I've got this odd feeling I might be interrupting her, although interrupting what, I don't know. It's as though she's started something that she hasn't quite finished, and I'm beginning to feel that I'm not the only one who needs to get something off my mind. You shouldn't feel so alone, she goes on, almost dreamy. There was a lot more of it going on than you might care to think, and as she says it she gives her shoulders a little shrug, nothing much, but enough to be noticed, and she takes her eyes off the window and meets my stare for a moment. But this time the hard look has gone from her eyes and there's something else there — I know she's showing me another part of her. What's more, I get the clear impression she doesn't show this bit off all that often, that what I've said has stirred something in her, and when she's finished, when she's done telling me that there was a lot more of it going on than I'd care to think, she just nods quietly to herself.

Because I don't know what to say, and because I'm not even sure if she wants me to say anything, I just sit there and I nod back. But from her manner I can see that she's not telling me this because she knows it from the helping work she does around the neighbourhood. No, this knowledge that there was a lot more of it going than you'd think is coming from somewhere else altogether. And I know I couldn't have come to a better woman with my little secret, the one that made me sick with worry and dragged me all the way here, because this good woman knows a few things about secrets like mine. That's when I look around this grand house of hers — its many rooms and the five daughters whose heads it puts a roof over — with a different eye.

When the time comes we put her good china cups aside and rise. She takes me to the door and I see Rita — looking more like a girl in her mother's house than she's ever looked before — hanging about at the end of the long, dark hall. Don't give it another thought, says her mother. And she's got that hard look in her eyes again, and again I know it's not for me. It's just to let me know that she's got it and knows when to use it, and that no one will know that doesn't need to know, because she won't have it.

As I'm walking back through the park, the same elms and gums and lawns have got a Sunday look they didn't have a few hours before when I marched along these shaded paths with this thing, this stain inside me that made me so sick it drove me out of the house. That's all gone. Now, on the grand day, I can watch them all — but not too close — and I'll know that nobody will know anything of what's been said who doesn't need to know, because that good woman won't have it.

From here, from this bed, it's all another life now, another age. Tomorrow is another year. Already, another year. I can hear them all laughing, out there in the yard. With their glasses, and their beer, and their funny little sparkling wines, they're laughing in the New Year. Those wonderful, young people. I hear it all, the way you do on hot, open nights like these, and I'm tempted to get up and join them, and I might. A cool glass of beer, and a laugh. They're just what I need.

16.

Miss Universe

A dream might look like this, if you could snap a dream and look at it the way you do at a photograph.

Under a clear, starry night the television sits on the lawn facing the street. The armchairs and easychairs from the lounge room have been placed on the lawn as well, facing back towards the lounge room from which they came. Likewise the coffee table and the lampshade. In the heavy, summer heat, the house has turned itself inside out. The private life of the house is on display: what they eat, what they say — and sound never seems to carry so well as it does on clear, summer nights — what they choose to watch on the television, who their guests are, what they drink and how much of it they drink.

It is a spectacle housed within a spectacle — a family on their front lawn, there to be observed as they themselves observe the shifting black-and-white images on the television.

All along the street, on this New Year's Eve, under the heavy night air, the houses have turned themselves inside out. The contents of their lounge rooms, kitchens and bedrooms have tumbled onto the front lawns like toys from a toy box. Televisions flicker amongst the shrubbery, mattresses have been dragged from bedrooms and children bounce in the moonlight. Laughter, telephones and the rattle of distant trains all hang in the air as if the sounds of the night are themselves too weary with the heat to move. Everybody's lives are on display, but only the school headmaster and his wife — who live in the next street and are embarking on their regular evening walk — seem to notice.

And Michael, who is sprawled on his stomach in a far corner of the lawn. He watches them too — his parents, their friends, as they drink their beers, their shandies, their sparkling wine and their lemonade. They are engine drivers, all of them, past and present, retired and still working. They talk of what they did, what they do, and how it's not the same any more. Even from where he is, Michael can see the sweat on his father's face, the sweat on all their faces, all the men, because they sweat, this bunch.

The first hint of summer, a big laugh, the slightest effort, and they sweat. A lifetime of standing in front of furnaces, of stoking fires to the point where the heat they emit can drive hundreds of tons of metal and wood, might do that to someone. Might just leave the pores of the skin permanently open so that the slightest effort, or a laugh — and they laugh with their whole body, these people — is enough to bring on a good, satisfying sweat. Although his father doesn't work any more, he sweats as if a lifetime of working habits, habits that he just can't break — like waking at five in the morning — are all still with him.

On and on they go, about their engines and their beer and their golf. Michael loathes all their talk. He loathes their beer that smells like vomit, and all their talk about it being the best beer in the world. All their stupid talk about — what is it again? — hops. And colour. He hears it every time his father's friends visit. Just as he hears all about their golf — their Gary Players and their Arnie Palmers. He can just see them all, on the fairway with their silly little gloves that have no fingers and their nine irons with Sam Snead scrawled across them and their spiked Gary Player golf shoes. They talk about them — these famous golfers — as if they're gods that just happen to be personal friends, as if they're all on first-name terms — and all because Arnold Palmer played at the club one Saturday the previous spring. The great Arnold Palmer strode across the lawns of the club to the first tee and hit the ball into oblivion. His father and all his friends stood by the edge of the tee and watched the ball disappear. And when he'd finished, when the great Arnold Palmer had finished his eighteen holes with a club record score, when he strode back to the clubhouse, he shook the hands of his father and his friends, and from that moment on he was always Arnie. He had tossed his Spalding Dot number 1 into the air when he'd finished and Michael watched a group of young caddies clamber for the ball that Arnold Palmer had hit. Ever since then the talk has been about how good he was with the kids, this Arnie of theirs.

Golf. He loathes it and all talk of it. He lays quietly on the grass and keeps his loathing to himself. Besides, they have stopped all their talk about golf and beer and engines. They are talking about the most beautiful woman in the world. Michael studies them, and their wives, as they all in turn watch the television. On the screen black-and-white figures come and go. Women in gowns. Bright gowns, subdued gowns. They step forward, they smile, they speak briefly, they turn and return to their places. But it is the woman with the silver crown in her hair and the dark sash across her chest who occupies the screen. This woman is Miss

Universe. As Michael rolls from his stomach onto his back, mentally playing with the images on the screen, he looks beyond the garden to the street and notices that all the televisions, on all the other front lawns, all contain the same image.

He returns his gaze to his front garden, to his parents and their friends gathered round the small table with its snacks and beer bottles and ashtrays. Everybody agrees that it is a good thing, a fine moment, that this woman — the most beautiful woman in the world — is ours. Her name — it is true — looks and sounds like the names of the Ukrainian family opposite, or like that of Michael's Polish friend down the street. But she is ours, and everybody nods that it is a good thing. There is a silence, then someone suggests it's a pity, though, that she isn't really one of us. Silently nodding, everybody agrees. It's a pity, this driver friend of his father's adds — encouraged by the general agreement — that she isn't a real Australian. This is what he meant to say, and he finally says it. Again everybody agrees that it is a pity, the nodding beginning all over again. It is good; no one suggests it isn't a good thing that this woman is now the most beautiful woman in the world. But it is a pity all the same.

The world will hear of this woman, and, through her beauty, they will hear of us. But they will all know that she isn't really one of us, her name will tell them that. From her name they will know — as surely as everybody else gathered in the front garden knows — that her beauty comes from a place other than here; and in their hearts, the rest of the world will wonder if this place can produce a thing of beauty all by itself. All agree, as the most beautiful woman in the world fades from the television screen, that their pride is lessened. In the darkness, those invisible figures somewhere out there in the rest of the world will see this woman of now-famous beauty and quietly notice that the seeds of her beauty lie elsewhere.

The men in their white shirts, in their golf shirts, the women in their floral dresses or their summer slacks, all return to their drinks — their squat beer mugs, their bright red, lipsticked glasses and their cigarettes. His mother switches the television off. Their talk continues. Soft, then loud with laughter, then soft again. Then a friend of his father's — a driver who takes the big passenger trains to the border and back again — swings round on his seat and notices Michael sprawled in his corner of the garden, where he'd been sprawled all night, and asks him what he is doing there. And Michael says 'nothing', because he isn't doing anything, and his father's friend nods as the whole gathering turns to face him: his father with a pleased, drunken beam across his face, his mother with a quiet smile, the rest of the gathering eyeing the boy slowly, all knowing full well that 'nothing' wasn't quite the word.

Then his father's friend speaks to him again.

'Well, come on. What do you think?'

Michael is confused, with everybody now staring at him.

'About what?'

'What do you think?' his father's friend grins. 'Is she beautiful?'

Michael shrugs, wondering if it shows, this loathing of them all and their stupid questions.

'How should I know?'

'Well, do you fancy her?'

Michael's mother speaks up.

'He doesn't think like that.'

'Oh, doesn't he just?' the wife of his father's friend says, leaning back in an easychair. 'He gave me quite a kiss — that boy of yours — when we got here.'

There are smiles and quiet laughter, and with the television off they are now watching Michael. He turns his head away and sees their cat perched on a neighbour's roof, indifferent to everything, and he is filled with an admiration for the cat that he can't muster for anybody or anything else around him.

'Is she one of us or not?' his father's friend continues.

Michael says he doesn't know, perhaps a little too quickly. Then he rises from the lawn and says that he is going for a walk. Where to, his father asks, and he says he doesn't know. His father's friend suggests that he doesn't seem to know much tonight and someone else says leave him alone. The last voice he hears, as he steps out onto the street, is his mother saying don't be long.

As he is leaving he sees the white, ghostly figure of his grandmother drifting across the lawn to the party, that faraway look in her eyes that is often there, as if in her mind she's living in another time. The party of friends has turned towards her and is transfixed by the sight of this late guest drifting towards them in the night. She has a chamber-pot in her hand. It is her way. When she empties the chamber-pot, she stops and talks to whoever is around, in whatever room of the house she may find herself, before returning to the room that was once his. His father is immediately uncomfortable. Michael can tell that from his face, for his father is never sure what his mother will say. She is a woman who likes an audience and who says things in public that make his father uncomfortable. Michael watches as his grandmother sits at a vacant chair, how she adopts the stiff-backed posture of a queen of somewhere or other, soaks up the greetings of his father's friends and immediately takes the stage as the unease settles into his father's features. Michael hears the words 'happy', 'hot' and 'New Year'. Then he hears the word 'Menzies' and watches, fascinated, as, stiff-backed in her chair, like royalty that was never summoned to the throne, she prepares to speak.

'Ah,' she says, pausing and looking round at everyone, judging her moment, knowing full well they are now hanging on her word. 'Menzies, that giant, immovable tree, whose' — and here she smiles sweetly — 'shall we call it shadow or shade, hangs over us all.'

She has them, this grandmother of his who likes an audience, with her sweet old lady stare and her faraway eyes that don't miss a thing. Michael leaves behind a shifting, moving, talking, group portrait. He moves away, slowly, under the darkness of his street, the front yards and houses all around him bright with porch lights, improbably placed lampshades and televisions flickering in the shrubbery. As he passes the houses of the street he instinctively falls into the ritual of his daily roll-call, as he would if going to or returning from school.

As the names of the houses automatically roll off his tongue, he tries to remember if he has ever asked that question: if they are our names, or their names. At the end of the street, just before the dip in the road that leads down to Bedser's, he turns to take in those distinct squares of light that represent each of the houses in the street. Each of them open to the night, but closed in with fences and gates. He continues walking and thinks of the Home and what Kathleen Marsden might be doing right now. If he went to the Home and softly called her name from the garden, would she hear? And if she heard, would she answer? And if she did, what would he say?

And then, somewhere in the country darkness of the hills and paddocks beyond the suburb, he swears he can hear music. Metallic music, island music. Rolling inexorably towards the suburb and his street, its very nature announcing that it comes from faraway places, where things are done differently.

As the music mounts, as its waves of sound roll irresistibly through the darkness, he knows that it brings with it those faraway places, and that, once here, a part of those faraway places will always stay behind. That from this point on there will be a before and an after, and this summer will be the boundary line by which such befores and afters will be measured.

17.

Joe Solomon's Cap

It is like being washed down a drain. Once you are in the middle of the crowd there is no going back, and Michael — feeling as though he has no more substance or motive power than a chewing gum wrapper — is swept on to the turnstile where a man in a grey dustcoat takes his ticket and spins him into the dark, concrete caves of the ground where everybody still seems sleepy and slow from their New Year's parties.

One long thoroughfare circles the entire ground. Occasional shouts, laughter and cries bounce sharply from wall to bare concrete wall, just above the constant, swirling hum of the crowd. Already, mid-morning, there are drunks propped up against the walls of this city-within-a-city, and the toilets are

118

jammed with people. As Michael and the crowd flow by, the sour scent blows over them, mingling with the smells of pies, hotdogs and spilt beer. All around him people walk with small transistor radios pressed to their ears, and the static and crackle of a thousand tiny speakers floats on this dark, humming river.

It is only when he sees the white number 12 on the bare concrete wall, that he gathers the will and strength to break from the flow, stepping over the butts, empty cigarette packets and discarded food scraps that have already begun to carpet the walkway, and up into the glare of the hot, morning sun. It is almost like being born for it is only at this point that Michael comes alive. The cool, cavernous darkness is washed away by the glare of the sun and Michael narrows his eyes as he looks up. And then the moment that never ceases to take his breath away, that sudden wave — not even a wave, the swell under the heart that passes through him every time — as the bright-green expanse of the playing field is suddenly spread out before him. Every time, he lingers just that bit longer than the crowd will tolerate, and he hears the complaints behind him as he pauses at the top of the stairs and takes in the green wonder of the place. Here the world opens out. Here the world is wide again. Here, whatever it is that he rolls up into a red leather ball and hurls down a narrow pitch as fast as he possibly can, is released.

Michael stumbles out into the day and allows the crowd behind him to spill into the seats and the standing-room sections of the arena. He dwells on the playing field, the smooth, green wonder of the thing. It is smooth and green like the pop-up cardboard games of Test Cricket in the shops or the playing fields on the covers of books; as smooth and unreachable as the playing fields in dreams, yet only a few yards away. Here the world opens out, here the world is wide again. Here the small eyes of the street, the chattering houses, the eyebrows that are raised all around him whenever his practice ball snaps into the back fence and resounds around the neighbourhood like a rifle shot, fade into insignificance. He sits in the only place on earth to which he knows he can bring his dreams and be certain that the place will take them in.

The heat is everywhere. Soon the ground will fill, but not even the crowd will absorb the heat. The sun is already high, and the clear invisible heat that is all around them hits the concrete paving at Michael's feet then rises up at him again because the sun hits you twice here. There is no breeze, no fresh air, just the same air, heated twice, moving round the ground, past the scoreboard, the shaded stand of the members, and back to the outer again. The trick is to forget the heat. When the white-hatted umpires and the players stroll out onto the wide green disc of the oval he concentrates on putting names to them all. The morning, the midday, the early afternoon all pass slowly.

Then, in the mid-afternoon heat, Michael takes his eyes off the game for a moment and everything becomes strangely quiet. Puzzled, he wonders how it is that so many people can make so little sound and so little movement. His eyes sweep the ground behind him, beside him, in front of him and back again, but he can neither see movement nor hear sound. It is a moment that needs explaining — that second that Michael's eyes left the ground and were not watching the play. As much as he looks for the reason in the crowd it isn't there. For in that second in which he took his eyes off the playing field, the cap of Joe Solomon fell from his head at the completion of a stroke, landed upon the stumps, and dislodged a bail. One bail, silently shifted from its groove at the top of the stump, fell — that's all it takes. Quite possibly everybody in the ground saw this except Michael. Michael heard only the silence of the crowd and saw only its stillness. At the same time, the crowd had witnessed only Joe Solomon's cap fall onto the stumps, but had no idea that it had collectively held its breath for a split second, become utterly still and silent and united in its breathlessness — only Michael saw that. The crowd, numbered later that day at 65,372 people, witnessed the fall of Joe Solomon's cap with great alarm and sadness. And the silence that occasions the fall of Solomon's cap and the subsequent dislodging of the bail, is a silence of deep concern. The eyes of the crowd move from the fallen cap — now lying on the ground as if having fallen in battle — to the Australian captain. He can, this crowd collectively knows, do one of two things: he can do the right thing, or he can do the wrong thing. And the crowd, in that overwhelming silence that so puzzles Michael because he has missed all of this, is holding its breath waiting to see what the Australian captain decides.

As Michael turns back to the playing field, now realising that the reason for this overwhelming silence is to be found out there, he hears the silence break. From the outer to the members, from the stalls to the dark, cool caverns of the numbered bays where even the drunks were quiet and still for that split second, the crowd is as one. And the one, crushing wave of sound it releases is as strange in Michael's ears as the silence that preceded it. This is not a happy sound. This is not the sound of spontaneous celebration which erupts from the crowd whenever a wicket falls. These are boos. All around Michael, this crowd is booing and jeering, and it is only when he stands with the crowd and follows the eyes and outstretched arms of those around him, that he realises they are booing the Australian captain. He had two choices, and now Michael stands in silence and watches as the crowd tells him that he chose badly.

For the rest of the afternoon the Australian captain lost his first name, in the same way that Jardine and Larwood lost theirs. He was, in the mind of the crowd, no longer Richie Benaud or even Richie, as he might have been referred to in more affectionate moments. He had simply become Benaud — and he stayed that way all afternoon.

On the orange, gravel path that leads out of the railway station and down into the Old Wheat Road, the world becomes small again. The boos and hisses of the afternoon still swirl round in Michael's head, just as, earlier that day, they had swirled round the vast, concrete stage of the MCG. Had he examined the faces in the crowd more thoroughly, he might well have seen variations of Mr Younger, Bruchner, Barlow and Webster — faces as familiar as those he sees daily in the street — all transformed by the moment. For that crowd had not only booed the Australian captain — they had done something far more serious — they had deprived him of his Christian name. They had denied him his citizenship for the afternoon, turned him into the other side, and turned the other side into theirs.

Michael is not someone who cares for the crowd. He doesn't have the gift of getting on with the crowd, unlike his father. It is a gift that Michael doesn't want. But today he saw and heard another crowd. That vast, concrete stadium they all shared that afternoon, it occurs to him as he strolls down the Old Wheat Road, is a place where the Bruchners and the Barlows and the Youngers and the Websters of this world can be bigger or smaller than they really are. And today when they rose from their seats as Joe Solomon's cap had so carelessly fallen from his head, onto the stumps, to dislodge his off bail, they rose like a people whom the summer had opened up. The summer, the music, tin drums and those surnames and place names that spoke of faraway lands, had opened up something in this crowd to the extent that they could make the other side theirs.

Michael stops at the top end of his street and absorbs the sights and sounds of the houses preparing for the evening. The world is small again, everybody back inside their houses. But for a short time that day, the careless hat of Joe Solomon had moved this quiet suburban world in ways that it hadn't counted on being moved when it woke up this morning. It had nudged their doors so that, even if they couldn't be called open to whatever is out there in the great world, their doors were — for a short time at least while the Australian captain was deprived of his Christian name — ajar.

Part Three

Monday, 16TH January 1961

18.

Frank Worrell Alone

He does not hear the noise of the crowd or the chat of his team. With his pads on, his gloves and bat by his side, Frank Worrell sits perfectly still in the team room looking out onto the ground. He hears none of the excited sounds around him. No one speaks to him. He is padded up, the next to bat, and he is concentrating on what he must do. So utterly concentrated that he is perfectly still and deaf to everything around him. So still, in fact, that he might be meditating, or even in a trance.

Throughout the tour he has learnt to think like a fly walking on water. He has learnt to walk upon the surface tension of the moment without breaking it. His mind is utterly concentrated. Frank Worrell is almost somewhere else. His body is in his seat overlooking the playing field of the Sydney Cricket Ground but his mind is elsewhere. His eyes, unblinking, look beyond the spectacle in front of him, and his head is turned slightly to one side as if receiving a communication from far away.

As he sits and waits for his time to stand and take his place on the playing field, he is contemplating the perfect stroke. He is not a person given over to too much contemplation of such matters, especially not during this tour, but at this moment he is dwelling on an image of perfection. A player is resting on one knee after completing the perfect cover drive. He sees the stroke in slow motion, the ball approaching, the front foot of the batsman advancing down the pitch, the moment of impact, the follow-through, and the right knee of the batsman coming to rest on the pitch as he watches the ball disappear. It is, he knows, a contemplation of the ideal, a moment that lives only in the mind, in that world of ideals that exists somewhere out there beyond the possibilities of this actual world.

At least, that is how he first sees it. But as he sits, in perfect stillness, he realises that the player is not anonymous, a stranger or a photograph of some famous figure from the past forever lodged in his memory. No, what he realises, with a jolt, is that he is watching an image of himself. And with this comes the feeling that although the stroke had not yet descended from the ideal to the actual world, it might soon do so. The part of Worrell's mind that was aware of events out there on the playing field has ceased paying attention, and Worrell is now utterly oblivious to the actual world. His mind moves on silence. The world around him is still and mute while he is in contact with this other one. He sits, impassive, convinced that an event that has already been played out is moving towards them all, and an act complete in all its intricate details is simply waiting for its time to enter the world of action on the wide, green playing field in front of him.

If he were a poet he might call this inspiration. A writer, he speculates, has such moments and then writes them down. The writing is an attempt to recover the moment of inspiration in which everything that is to be written arrived, complete in its detail. It may take a day, a year or a decade. Frank Worrell has only today.

When the world returns and he is once more conscious of everything around him, he tells no one. He is not that kind of person. Not the kind to talk when talk is not required. Besides, Frank Worrell is alone. He has been alone all through the summer and he will stay that way until the summer ends.

To share this moment would be to break the surface tension, and his mind would no longer be moving on silence. If he were to speak of it he would surely awake and find only air and space beneath his feet. It is all part of being alone. As he rises from his seat, as he picks up his gloves and his bat and walks towards the door that will lead him out onto the ground (his turn to bat has come), Frank Worrell is filled with the inexplicable conviction that a stroke, perfect in all its detail, has already been completed, that it is moving steadily towards him, and that it will join him out there on the playing field.

19.

Webster at Work

I t is the noise of the factory that he loves most of all. He is quite happy to call it a noise, for it is no more a sound than a smell is a scent. Webster is at home with the noise of his factory. The thump of the hammers of the giant new machines, the sound of sheet metal being crushed into shape, the clatter of bolts and engine parts dropping into trays so that they might be boxed and sent to other factories, the raised voices of the machinists shouting over the din, and the metallic echo of the loudspeaker rising over it all with directives for so-and-so at assessments or storage to report to the office ... This is the world Webster made and these are its noises — full of life and energy and purpose. Without this sense of order, of organised industry that comes with the noise, the whole thing would be a mere din. A chaotic racket.

Webster has always been invigorated by this noise, because he brought it to the suburb. It is *his* noise. It stirs him like music. Or, it always has. This morning, a hot and sticky Monday, he is sitting in his office on a mezzanine floor overlooking the factory. His tea and a pale biscuit are sitting on the desk. The sliding windows have been pushed open and the noise enters the makeshift room of his office unimpeded. Webster sits back in his seat, barely seeming to register either the sights or sounds of the place. He is perfectly still. He has lost track of time. His eyes blank, he rises from his seat and slides the windows shut. The volume drops instantaneously and the factory is muffled.

Neither the noise, nor the sights, nor smells of the place stir him this morning. With dull eyes he surveys the factory floor and wonders who everybody is — even though he is normally proud to say he knows the names of all his employees. This sensation is not new, but the recurrence of it is more frequent. It is, he suspects, similar to that feeling that husbands and wives have when they look at a loved one and suddenly realise they don't love them any more, or never did. Except, in Webster's case, it is not so dramatic. He has merely had long-held doubts confirmed. He's doing what he does best, and will continue to do so. To do otherwise, he is convinced, would be an impractical waste of a life. He just doesn't love what he does any more.

At first he took it as a phase, this falling out of love. He is, Webster knows, one of those people who is defined by what he does. His factory is not just a job, a vocation, something that can be picked up, dropped and swapped afterwards when the thrill is gone. Throughout the suburb, he knows, he is simply referred to as Webster the factory. He *is* this place. It is his monument.

Without explanation and with only the most perfunctory of farewells, he rises from his seat, leaves his office and walks out of the factory. At home he spends the rest of the morning in his grounds talking to the gardeners, helping them move shrubs in the sticky heat. Mistakes had been made in the winter planting and shrubs too delicate to withstand the summer had to be moved to more shaded areas of the grounds. One of the gardeners has his transistor strung from a handle of the wheelbarrow and the cricket follows them wherever they go. It is pleasant work, and it is good to be in close contact with the gardens and grounds that he rarely sees close up or pays such detailed attention to. It is also good to be sweating. He joins in discussion about the state of the game, something he rarely does because it has never interested him.

He even pauses in silence when the commentators speak of a stroke that has just been played by the West Indian captain. It is, they are saying, perfect in all its detail. As Webster listens to their descriptions of the moment and its perfect detail, there is something disturbingly familiar about it all, as though in some odd part of his mind he has already witnessed the stroke and experienced the moment before coming to the garden and experiencing it all over again. At such moments his own mind is a complete mystery to him. There are, in fact, times out there in the garden when he quite forgets who he is. Then he remembers. He is Webster. Webster the factory. And with that he remembers that his whole interior echoes because something isn't there any more. That he echoes, like a large house that has been emptied of its furniture.

That evening, the air still warm, the night sky extraordinarily clear, the drone of the crickets all around him, Webster sits in a cane chair under the lights of the verandah and contemplates the garden he worked in that afternoon.

When this feeling of the utter uselessness of everything first came over him, he shrugged it off. He kept on working in his factories and his passion for the work remained with him. But the feeling came back again and again, until he couldn't shrug it off. Now his passion for this game of his, this game that had been his life — of producing small objects that eventually became part of large objects that are useful to people — is gone.

Outside the self-contained world of his mansion, the residents of the suburb are tossing and turning in restless summer sleep. But Webster's restlessness doesn't come from the summer heat. Webster's restlessness will still be with him in the cool of the morning, in the autumn and winter, when the leaves of the peach and apple trees are mulch on the garden beds, when the fruit has been peeled and eaten and the pips spat out. No, Webster smiles for the first time all evening, if only his restlessness could be put down to the summer heat.

20.

Shame

New walls. White walls. I never dreamt I'd find myself in such a room. There's something about white walls. Always has been. There's something about white. Always good to have it around you. Lots of white. You don't need pictures on white walls. You don't need fixtures. All those useless things that hang around a house, making everything dark and gloomy. And big windows. Such windows. That's all a white wall needs, windows like these.

My hip is better now, just from being here. If only this throat would go. But that's the worst of summer colds. They hang about forever. Thank God, thank Jesus, Mary and Joseph, thank the man who grows the hops, and the malt and barley, who gives it to the man who stirs the brew and gives us beer. The beer that Rita keeps cool in the refrigerator — no ice box, mind you — and gives to me. She comes to me like an angel, twice a day, with a tall glass of cool beer, and waits until I've sipped it empty because my throat's not so good. I've never been one to sip beer. Beer wasn't made to be sipped. Beer was made to be drunk, but these days I sip the stuff. God bless you, Rita, I say, as she hands me the stuff that cools my throat. While I'm sipping it I look over the rim of the glass and I watch her eyes as she tells me about the street, this white-wall suburb of theirs, Vic, and young Michael, who seems to do nothing but hurl cricket balls through the air. And the more I see of Rita, and we get to see a lot of each other because she's often here looking out for me, the more I see she's not a girl any more. Not the girl I remember who was going out with my Vic, because he'd always been my Vic. But from the moment she entered the house I knew he'd become her Vic. I got over it. They say you don't, some types, but you do. You get over these things and you find something else to do with your life. She was so young. She was a girl, but when I look over the rim of the glass and into her eyes I see she's not a girl any more. Not the girl she was when I sat in that house in South Melbourne where Vic and I lived, when I sat there till I couldn't stand sitting there any more. When I sat in that tiny house in South Melbourne and looked at its dark walls, till I couldn't stand it any more. Till the shame drove me out of that gloomy house and propelled me right across the wide, spring gardens, in my best clothes — because it was a Sunday — walking all the way under the plane trees, and the elms and the gums of that park that had never seemed so wide as it did that day because I never thought I'd reach that grand house in Tivoli Street where Rita and her mother and her sisters lived. Walking all the way, with my head down, wringing my hands, wondering what on earth I could say when I got there except for the truth. So, even though I had all that time to prepare something to say, I just got there and fell into a chair in front of Rita's mother — with Rita in another room, because this was women's talk — and I said Ivy, I can't stand it any longer. I'm sick with it. With this shame. And I told her it all. As I was telling her, it all came back to me — the shame of being packed off in the country dark so no one would see me all those years ago, but only yesterday. In the dusk. Cold and clear and damp. Old shame never goes away.

I remember a long, low cloud, orange and purple, the plain low and flat and going on forever, whichever way you looked. There was a touch of spring in that cloud, and in the low sun sinking into the wheat fields just beyond the farmhouse. Why did there have to be? It was winter and I remember a touch of spring and feeling good for the first time in weeks. My bag was on the back of the cart, and everything I had was inside it — clothes, letters, and little bracelets and rings I'd carried around with me all my life. And a book. There was always a book, which I read at the railway station and on the train. What was it? It doesn't matter now. It kept me company, I remember that much, and now it's gone. But it did its job and took my mind off things for a day. I call that a good book.

It took my mind off that low cloud, the low fields and the farmhouse I was leaving. It took my mind off it all. That, and the touch of spring that shouldn't have been there, and the moment of happiness that came with it that shouldn't have been there either. We followed the damp, dirt road to the town, and by the time the farmhouse was small and I could see enough of the fields to make out different squares of green and yellow while the sky turned dull, my moment of happiness passed. That's it. That's all you get today, old girl, I said. And I wasn't that old, but there I was calling myself old girl anyway. Then one of those low hills that creeps up on you suddenly took the view away — the fields, the trees, the farmhouse, the whole estate — and I never saw that view again.

You hear stories about girls who get themselves in trouble and you think poor silly thing, or just shrug it off because it's someone else and you've got a lot to do besides. Suddenly that someone else was me, and even then on that cart, being packed off in the dusk — cold and clear and damp — I could hear a chorus of poor silly thing being muttered by friends and strangers alike, when the news finally got out on the farm, in the town, and back at home in the city where I was heading.

The sun went from the sky, that touch of spring left the air, and it wasn't dusk any more, it was dark. I had fifty pounds in my purse. A lot of money in those days. Viktor, that was his name, Viktor placed a shawl around my shoulders because I didn't have one, and said, here's fifty quid. You know you can't stay, and he said it all sad and slow, his eyes pleading — here's fifty quid. And I looked at the fifty pounds, all rolled up in one-pound notes, and it was a weighty roll of notes, I could see that. He held it out for an eternity, saying here's fifty quid, you know you can't stay. And I looked at that roll of notes in his hand on the end of his extended arm, and I thought ... if I take it, if I take it ... what am I? And all the time his arm was held out and he was saying, you're going to need it, his eyes all sad with that brooding look Vic eventually took on when he was old enough to know what a dad was and that he didn't have one when everybody else did. God knows what he said in the playgrounds when they asked him, because he never told me. He just brought that glum look back into the house and it never left him. I hadn't yet seen that look in my boy's face because he wasn't born then, that night I sat up on the cart and left in the dark. But when it came into his eyes and into our house I knew it was his father's glum look, the one that Viktor had on his face the night he held out his hand to me. And so I'm staring at this roll of notes thinking … if I take it, if I take it, what am I? Then I took it, and a smile lit up his face because I'd just washed his hands of the whole affair. The shawl was for my shoulders, the fifty pounds was for my silence. The fifty pounds was for his peace of mind. It went a long way, that fifty pounds.

That was how I said goodbye to the estate (and it's still there, Viktor's dead, the son's a mayor). The cart took forever to get into town, and I kept on wishing the driver — who gave me one look and a quick nod before climbing onto the seat — would speed up and get me there. But why? What was I in such a hurry to get to? I wanted to get away, so the shame of being packed off in the night would become a memory, the way these things do. Become a memory and get old and go away. But it didn't. It's still there, even now, cold and clear and damp.

Here she comes, my little angel. The door is open. The daylight streams in, the cricket crackles on out there in the kitchen. Here she comes, my little angel. The girl's gone from her eyes all right, but she looks like an angel with that tall glass in her hands. Here, she's saying, take this, it'll cool you down and soothe that throat of yours. There's nothing worse, she says, than a summer cold on a hot day.

21.

Kathleen Marsden Alone

Finding a place to yourself is easier in summer. In winter, in the crowded Home, it is impossible. But in summer the garden of the Home has shaded corners that you can lose the world and gather yourself in. If someone sees you tucked away in one of those shaded corners, they'll leave you be in summer because they'll know you've gone there to be alone. While Frank Worrell is seated in his chair overlooking the playing field of the Sydney Cricket Ground, and while Webster sits dull-eyed in his factory, Kathleen Marsden has come to one of those shaded corners of the garden to be alone.

There are different ways of being alone. Kathleen Marsden is sixteen and knows this already. There is a part of Kathleen Marsden that has always been alone, and known that there is no one to whom she is connected in the way that children with parents and brothers and sisters are connected. A part of Kathleen Marsden has been alone all her life, and that same part of her will remain alone forever. No matter how things may change in the future, there will always be the island that was Kathleen Marsden, the Kathleen Marsden who knew only herself and relied only on herself. It is not something she is sad or angry about any more; it is simply something she knows, this particular way of being alone.

This morning, sitting in one of those shaded corners of the garden, she is alone in another way. A way that she likes, for she has withdrawn from the Home, its noise and children and chatter, because she wants to. The first way of being alone is a result of having been thrown into the world, it is a way of being alone over which you have no say. You are thrown, you land, you look about and there is nothing to which you feel connected. There is you and you alone. But this morning Kathleen Marsden has not been thrown into her shaded corner of the garden, as she was into life, rather she has taken herself there with the intention of being alone. It is a section of the garden to which she comes often in summer, and over the years the other girls have learnt to leave her be when they see her there. Only the young ones seek her out.

But this morning they don't. No one does. She has the place to herself, a patch of lawn under one of the old elm trees of the district, where she can sit and think and gather herself. She has learnt this morning, as they all did in the breakfast hall, that the Home is to be shut down. It is the only home she has ever had and soon, very soon, it will close. They will all move to another Home miles from the suburb on the other side of the city, and once again this feeling of being thrown about is upon her.

Already she is looking upon the garden, the Home and its many rooms, like someone who will not be looking at them for much longer. And all the things that might once have bothered her — the sinking beds, the dull light of the downstairs rooms, the peeling wallpaper — are not a bother to her now. Although she never speaks of her love for this rambling old place that has been her home forever, it is there. It is one of the reasons she has come to this shaded corner of the garden — her love for this rambling old house (whose history she knows in the same way that one knows one's family history), and whatever it is she keeps in her heart for Michael. This other Michael she only just discovered. She has known him since they were children, and now they are beginning to know each other in different ways. In the last few weeks they have crossed a shadowy line that neither of them knew was there until they crossed it; a line that marked the end of their childhood ways of knowing each other and marked the beginning of this other knowledge. In those few weeks she has noted those first, wondrous feelings that come with being connected. It is as though a whole new order of feeling is being born inside her. A birth that makes her giddy, and light-headed; a feeling, she imagines, like the effect of alcohol. She has begun to feel, for the first time, that there really is someone out there after all. She is less thrown when she is with him, and although she can't bring herself to trust this feeling, she doesn't want to lose it, not yet. So, for this reason, she has decided not to tell Michael that the Home will soon be closed and that she will go to the other side of the city — which may as well be the other side of the world — when it does. For the first time in her life she has the feeling that there is someone out there after all, and she wants that feeling to stay, and for that feeling to stay everything around her must remain as it is. She wants everything to go on as if nothing has happened. Over the remainder of the summer she will live as though the world will not change, and she will not be thrown about once again, just when she thought she had landed.

In that shady corner of the garden where she sits — as Frank Worrell prepares to rise and meet his moment — sixteen-year-old Kathleen Marsden resolves to hold her world together over the remainder of the summer with her will, and live each day as though nothing changes.

22.

A Diesel at the Mill

Vic turns his cheek to the wind then looks down to the road passing by beneath him, at the wheels of Rita's bicycle spinning round, as he rides to the Old Wheat Road for the morning shopping. It is a familiar path, past the school, its red-brick classrooms quiet under the peppercorns, past the tennis courts, freshly raked and sprinkled, and up into the Old Wheat Road. It's an easy and pleasant ride — best taken in the mornings, before the sun bakes the suburb — and Rita's bicycle, never used by her, is as good as new and travels smoothly.

It wasn't really that long ago he regularly pushed Rita along Toorak Road and up the Tivoli Road hill. Not really that long ago, but long enough to be another life. Yet there are days and nights when he could swear that nothing's changed, and others when he's remembering the actions of somebody else whose name happens to be Vic. A different Vic. A Vic as separate from him as a character in a book or a movie, whose name might also be Vic. The years do that. The years were his. The years were his, and Rita's, and the boy's, and the years went quickly. All twenty of them. And you don't walk out on all those years just like that. But you can't keep this little number up all your life, either. Can you, Victor? he asks himself quietly as he enters the Old Wheat Road. Not so long ago it was like the main street of a wild west town, all weeds and dirt and long swaying grass. Now it's just like anywhere else. He parks his bicycle outside the butcher's and removes the clips from his trouser legs. You don't just walk out on twenty years.

But soon, before the years run out altogether, he will. Then they'll both have to start again. No longer Vic and Rita. No longer 'we' and 'us', but what they were before their lives merged and led them all the way out here to a world of neat new lawns and glistening weatherboard houses. To everybody else around him these are the streets they will live their lives in. Even the young families look old, like they've arrived at their stop and their journey is over.

Inside the butcher's he chats about golf, because the butcher is a mid-week golfer. And he plays like one. He swings his club like he's swinging a leg of lamb, and most of the time he may as well be. The cool smell of the shop rises up through the sawdust at Vic's feet, and he stares out the window at the greengrocer's opposite while taking in the sound of the butcher's meat cleaver. A few moments later the greengrocer weighs the onions that Vic will fry with the steaks he has just bought, then gently drops them into a brown paper bag as though they are semi-precious stones. The pharmacist hands him his new supply of pills and tells him — like he always does — that the pills are useless with grog. Vic smiles as he always does and takes the pills, and the pharmacist smiles as he passes them over. That's the other thing about the suburb, everybody knows what's going on.

Then, somehow, he's standing at the junction of the two main streets of the suburb, opposite the flour mill and the milk bar that's recently taken on the fancy name of The Rendezvous. The steaks, the onions and the pills are in his string bag, his bicycle is resting against his thigh, the clips are in his pocket. How did he get here? And how long had he been here? There was a sound, he remembers that, and a vague sensation of being called. But what called him? Whatever it was he answered the call and followed it as if he were walking in a dream, and part of him wonders if he's not having a turn. A small one, but enough to throw everything out of whack. But he's not. This is different. This is like being roused by some previous incarnation and he can't decide if he's been roused from a dream or is entering one. Then he hears it again, the thing that called him. Long and deep. Like it knew he was out there. He takes in the deep throb of the engine, the hiss of the Westinghouse brake, the power of the thing, this shunting diesel, as it effortlessly carries a line of trucks laden with grain along the service track that runs beside the mills, then out into the world of diesel and steam, where trains go on without him.

It's at times like these that he has to remind himself that he was a driver once, and that he drove, drank and walked with the best. He watches the diesel chugging away from the mills, and knows that the driver is a mug. He also knows that he, Vic, could get in the cabin even now, and drive that thing — a mere shunting diesel — the way it was born to be driven.

Then it's gone, and he's left at the junction holding the handlebars of Rita's bicycle with one hand and the string bag of shopping with the other. On the way back, through those quiet, trimmed streets, he notices that the players are out on the tennis courts, that the schoolyard is silent and snoozing through the holidays, and notes that the morning will be gone if he's not careful.

23.

Frank Worrell Went Down on One Knee

Vic doesn't know it, but while he was standing at the intersection of the Old Wheat Road and the main street, drawn to the diesel at the mill, gazing upon its familiar blue-and-yellow crest and listening to the ancient rumble of its engine, something perfect entered the world. Frank Worrell went down on one knee. In another suburb, in another city, but under the same sun and at exactly the same time, Frank Worrell went down on one knee and delivered into the world a perfect act — a perfect moment. A moment that was bigger than the whole of the year in which it took place because it will outlast it. A moment so perfect that years after Vic is no longer alive, years after the engine that he gazed upon is consigned to scrap and its ancient rumble silenced, people will talk of this act — the day Frank Worrell went down on one knee and drove Alan Davidson through the covers for four. Everything stopped at that moment — Davidson, Worrell, the players, the crowd, Michael with his head bowed over the plastic radio in the kitchen, and Vic at the intersection of the Old Wheat Road and the main street of the suburb. Everything stopped, except the ball. Oblivious of the nature of its going, the ball travelled majestically to the boundary. The batsman stayed resting on his knee, perhaps as oblivious of the perfection of the moment as the ball, or, more likely, reluctant to leave the stroke, knowing full well that he would never know such a moment again. Reluctant to leave this moment that he glimpsed back in the players' rooms, this moment that he knew was waiting for him out there on the playing field. But the moment was now leaving him, and would never come again. And the bowler, as still as the crowd around him, seems almost grateful to have played his part in the construction of a perfect act. Michael can only imagine this as he stands with his hands on the kitchen bench listening to the radio. But he knows something extraordinary has occurred because the stroke is followed by silence on the radio. There is a silence because the commentators cannot find the words to describe what they have just witnessed. That is what perfection does to people — even those who know the game and speak of it often and well. Even though he cannot see the face of Davidson, even though he will not see it until that evening when the stroke is shown on television — he can picture it. A part of him is convinced already that this is a moment — not only of perfection — but a moment in which rivalry becomes collaboration. Together, they have made this moment. And as much as Davidson wants Worrell's wicket, as much as he wants to see his stumps scattered across the ground, or — if not his wicket — as much as the bowler wants him unnerved and the stuffing knocked out of his bloody perfect composure — as much as he wants all this — Michael also knows that there must have been a moment when Davidson looked up from his follow-through, saw the stroke, and reached for the right words but, like the commentators on the radio, found only silence. Had he been less of a bowler the ball would not have been as good as it was. Michael looks at the delivery on television later that evening, and it is a good ball. Any less of a batsman and he would not have risen to the occasion and would not have found the stroke that was there waiting to be found. This shot was no accident. The bowler, the ball, the batsman, the bat, the heat, the breeze, the humidity — they all had the possibility of this shot written into them and, together, the bowler and the batsman found it.

No other moment in the remainder of the test will matter as much as this one stroke. Not the result, not the wickets that fell, or the runs that were gathered. Only this moment. That night in front of the television when he dwells on the shot and when he reads accounts of it in the evening newspaper, his faith — that something perfect *can* enter the ordinary world of streets and shops and trimmed lawns — is affirmed. And even those who don't care much for the game will have paused before their television screens in acknowledgment that this was an event. For Michael, all that matters is that someone has done it. Worrell may have imagined playing just such a stroke all his life, seen it in his mind's eye again and again, and always assumed that it would stay there — in his mind. Always assumed that perfection could not be taken out of the mind and placed in the actual world — that, like a particularly vivid dream, it would all dissolve on waking. But he has lived the dream, and it is documented — in print, photographs and on film. It is forever his — and everybody else's. With that thought, Michael considers that there may even have been a moment of sadness on the part of Worrell —

that when you live the dream, you lose the dream. That while the idea of playing the perfect shot remains a thought, it is always beckoning — and always belongs only to the dreamer, to be summoned up like a toy and played with, then dispatched when play is done. But when the dream and reality merge, it is not only finished, but belongs to everyone, for it has entered the world. And that might be sad. He fancies that this sadness might too be written into the shot, that as everything came together and Worrell could feel in his bones what he was about to do — in that split second when the player is privileged to feel the perfection of the moment before passing it on to the crowd — there was a deep sense of loss as well as giving. The stroke no longer lives in his mind, but has gone out into the world. As Worrell lingered on one knee, it is just possible he was trying to hold onto that moment a little longer, before losing it forever.

As Michael cuts the newspaper article out for his scrapbook that night, it occurs to him that they all bring their gifts to the game — speed, daring, cunning, danger. But Worrell's shot was something else. Worrell's shot was a poem, the sort of poem that his English teacher constantly hammers them with, after having laughingly called them all peasants. And as he sits at his desk wondering why he should call this shot a poem, the word 'grace' pops into his head and then out of it as he writes the word down on the page in front of him and looks at it. He's never thought about this word much before, and until now he's never really understood what it meant. Now he does. Worrell's stroke is a picture of grace. He now understands the word because he can picture it.

For Michael, the world outside, where days tumble into days, and months tumble into years without anybody breaking ranks during the march to and from the station, bus stop and tram stop, will be just that much better for having been momentarily distracted by it. This thing of distracting perfection has entered the world, just as one day Michael will distract the world with the perfect ball — which will, in time and beyond time, become known as the ball that Michael bowled. For the lesson of Frank Worrell's cover drive is that it can be done, after all.

Part Four

Saturday, 21st January 1961

24.

An Unfortunate Maturity

Michael is placing his cricket gear in his school bag. He is sitting on a small stool in the laundry at the back of the house. Vic is leaning in the doorway. It is a bright Saturday morning, bright on the green leaves and flowers of the garden, a gift of a morning. Vic is noting the care Michael takes in packing his bag and is wondering why he doesn't just throw everything in the way any kid would. But he doesn't. The white shirt, the pants, ironed the night before by Rita — the cap and the socks, are all carefully placed in the bag, folded one on top of the other like sheets in a linen press. Maids would have folded bed sheets like this in old houses, in that not-too-distant world when domestic staff, like his mother, folded the bed linen of the well-to-do with uncomplaining care, in that not-too-distant world in which his mother, and all their mothers, had paid for their futures, day after day, shift after shift, with the best hours of their lives. Now, with the Saturday nights that she never knew all gone, and with the future bought, she lies in bed and waits for the whole caper to end, her best hours given to people who never noticed. Those hours, Vic notes as he lounges in the doorway watching his son prepare for the day's cricket, were her gift. And she gave them knowing she would never see them again.

Michael's bat, in its vinyl sheath, sits beside the bag. He seems older than his years, thinks Vic. Except when he's throwing that ball down a cricket pitch. Not that Vic has seen him bowl much. Once, in fact. A year before. Rita took him to a match. He was standing on the boundary line watching the game, idly wondering who the bowler was — this bowler who seemed so tall and who ran so far before he even let the ball go — when he realised it was Michael. How could he not recognise his own son, whom he saw every day? But he hadn't. It was, he reasoned, the unfamiliar surroundings and the unusual company of cricketers. It was not until Michael had turned and walked back to his mark that his features became suddenly familiar. The thought that crossed Vic's mind then is the same thought that crosses it often these days. Where did he learn all this? Where did he learn to be what he is, a boy older than his years who doesn't need him, doesn't need any of them any more. Vic dwells on the sight of the boy who has grown while he was looking the other way, and it occurs to him that he must have been looking the other way for years. Michael, Vic notes, will organise his world in the same way that he organises his bag, layer upon layer. And having organised it he will learn to move through it in measured strides as he does on the field. The playing field, Vic is sure, is the boy's centre. Out there, he knows his world wholly. Vic saw it that day as clearly as he saw that the boy did not need him any more. He will take that air of certainty that he has out on the playing field with him wherever he goes. Know one world, Vic has always reasoned, and you will have the key to them all. Michael may or may not have reasoned this as well, he may have come to this conclusion intuitively. But it's where his confidence comes from. Vic envies him, envies him for this confidence that he never had, at his age or any other, and never will.

Vic looks around the laundry noting that he too once sat on the same stool and packed his work bag in the days when the room smelled of steam and cinders, when the smell of his overalls and faded caps brought the job into the house. There are times when he can still smell faint traces of his job, but the smell, of course, like the job, has gone. What he can smell at such times are his memories.

His bag packed, Michael remains hunched over it, staring intently at the contents as if something were missing but he can't fathom what. Vic is amused.

'What are you doing?'

Michael looks up slowly.

'I'm trying to imagine a time when I'm not here,' he says, nodding at the house. 'When you're not here, Mum's not here — and we're not us. It's not that difficult.'

He does this. He always does this. You ask him a perfectly innocent question and he does this. It is — at least this is the way Vic thinks of it — it is his unfortunate maturity. It's the reason why Michael doesn't need them any more, and it all happened while Vic wasn't looking.

'I'm getting myself ready,' Michael continues. 'I have been for years.'

Sensible, Vic thinks as his tongue clicks the roof of his mouth and he scans the yard ablaze with that special Saturday-morning sun. Very sensible. He's making sure he doesn't get hurt. He's been making sure for years. And although part of Vic wants to tell the boy to relax and just act his age, he is quietly pleased. Besides, he knows that the time for all that fatherly advice about acting his age and being the boy that he is, has long since passed.

It is then, still staring out across the yard, that Vic begins speaking as if he is internally rehearsing something important and speaking out loud at the same time.

'When you've grown. When you've gone to university, or working or doing whatever it is you've got your mind set on. I'll go.'

Michael nods without speaking, the gesture clearly saying that he knows this. That he has always known it.

'I've got a little fishing town picked out up north. When everything is finished here. I'll go there.'

Michael nods again, knowing that he will be as true as his word. Then Vic turns from the yard to Michael.

'This is just between us.'

Michael's eyes are steady.

'Why did you tell me, then?'

'Because this is a chat between you and me.'

Rita is shopping. Mary is sleeping. They have the house to themselves. It is, it seems to Vic, the time for a confidential remark.

'You won't tell?'

Michael closes his bag and looks up, shaking his head quietly, as the front door opens and Rita enters the house.

'No. But I don't see why I shouldn't. And I just might, anyway.'

Vic grunts in the doorway as Michael stands.

'You always do this, don't you? Both of you. You put me in the middle.'

Vic notes a look of disapproval in his son's eyes, a look that is there more often than Vic would like it to be, and he puts it down to the boy's unfortunate maturity. It is the reason why he doesn't need them any more. The reason why he doesn't need anyone any more. And that, Vic concludes, while Michael sits with the bag between his legs, is a good way to be.

25.

A New Way of Walking

Rita can hear the low murmur of their talk in the back of the house. She can't hear what they are saying, only the low, almost confidential nature of their talking. She is aware of it, like one is aware of music on the wireless when the wireless is low. She has been to the city this morning. She left early and went to the city because she wanted a dress of quality. You won't find a dress of quality in this suburb. She hears Michael's voice and sighs quietly, dwelling on the unfolding mystery of her son. Once, she mentally notes — happy at the bedroom mirror — it was the crack of that bloody ball against the back fence that drove her mad. Now it's his constant coming and going, with his bag over his shoulder. And that look in his eyes, like he doesn't notice anybody else any more. Maybe he doesn't.

Feel like I'm going to have to — she hums as the new dress falls over her — feel like I'm going to have to, what do they call it, pad up, to get his attention. He comes and goes. Always with that look in his eyes. And as the dress falls she hears him in the laundry, getting his things together so he can be gone, again. But why so soon? It is still morning, and already he is preparing to leave.

Rita is adjusting the straps of a new dress, a dress that, like all her dresses, is just a bit too good for the street. And the street will look, but who cares? It'll give the street something to look at, and it'll give those tongues, all the way down to poor old George Bedser's shuttered house, something to wag about. The street, she quietly hums to herself, can get stuffed. Although Rita is not a woman to tell anyone to get stuffed all that often, she's happy to address the street in this manner. The dress makes her feel good, and she gets into it easily, which makes her feel good too. She smoothes the light summer cotton over her hips then swings round from the bedroom mirror and walks down to the laundry — the measured, unhurried steps of a mature woman on the outside, the impatient heart of a girl within her.

'Well?'

She's standing in the doorway of the laundry. As she speaks Michael looks up from his bag. In the background she hears the clatter and rattle of Vic playing around with his bloody golf buggy. The golf course, that can get stuffed too. And all golfers. At first Michael's eyes barely register her presence, and once again she has the distinct impression that she ought to be carrying a bat and wearing pads to catch his attention. Then he eyes the dress, a little like the street would eye the dress, a little like a son who doesn't really think his mother should be wearing such a dress. It is not, the look suggests, a mother's dress. Not that it's daring, but it's stylish, and Rita paid for that style. There is disapproval in her son's eyes. Disapproval in his eyes when he's got the time to give it, that is. As she takes this in, she tries to locate its source. Tries to see her dress, herself inside the dress, from where he is sitting. And she wonders, for one tense moment, if it's happened, if she's crossed that shadowy line, and if her son is looking back at a mother who not only wears dresses that are a bit too good for the street, but that are now a bit too good for her. A bit too — and she drags the word out of her and silently utters it — a bit too young. Had she become, without knowing it, that object of embarrassment to young sons — the mother who draws attention to herself? The casual damning of the street, the balancing act of the mature woman's walk and the young girl's impatient heart that she felt so comfortable with a moment ago, the good feeling she had as she smoothed the light, summer cotton over her hips, evaporates, and she sees the dress for what it is — a stylish piece of work, but now meant to be worn by a younger woman.

'It's nice,' he finally says.

'You don't like it.'

'I do.'

'You think it's too young for your mother, don't you?'

'I don't. It's nice.'

Suddenly she's changing her mind and looking at the dress, at herself inside the dress, all over again.

'You don't have to say it.'

'I'm not. It's nice. Your dresses always are.'

For a moment, while she's changing her mind about the dress all over again, she remembers Michael, the little boy, lightly touching her new dresses when they came into the house and saying, 'Nice Mama, nice.'

She sees him again. Her little man in short pants who always gave her the green light to wear her dresses, and who always noticed when no one else did. He's still there, and for a moment she has to look away in case this chat they're having loses its light, casual tone. And what she took to be a look of disapproval in his eyes a moment ago is just the look that he wears now because his mind is always on other things; on banging that bloody cricket ball into the back fence or down a pitch.

Then his head is buried in the school bag once more, and the eyes that don't notice anybody or anything else are back. But it doesn't matter. The dress is good again, and the feeling she had as she smoothed the light summer cotton over her hips in front of the mirror is back. There is nearly always tension in the house, but not today. Today their talk is as light as the cotton dress that falls over her like a floral cloud.

It is the walk she notices. Or, the difference in the way of walking. A walk tells you a lot about someone — more than the words people speak or their gestures or their eyes. Walking can tell you more than anything.

Vic is always walking into an imaginary wind — and a cold one. It doesn't matter if it's winter or summer, it's always the same cold wind. It's always there because he brings it with him. Wherever he goes. And he's always looking about from side to side as he leans into his walk as if expecting to be mugged at any minute by another depression or another war, or some new disaster that he can't name, but which he's sure is out there anyway. Just waiting for its chance. It doesn't matter where he is, on the street, in the yard, at the shops. It's always the same.

But not Michael. He doesn't walk like that. And that's why she notices his walk. It's got bounce. He might have an old head, God knows he didn't have much choice but to grow up before his time, but he's got so much bounce in those steps of his that he seems to be walking on springs. He's not looking about while he's walking, or down at his feet, and he's certainly not looking back. This isn't a walk that is wary of the future, this is a walk that can't wait to get at it. And it's not just youth, is it? Vic was young once, but Rita can't believe he ever walked any differently. No, you learn to walk like Vic in hard times, and once the walk is learnt, it is never forgotten. But if you've never known hard times, if you've never felt the floor, the footpaths, the streets of your everyday life go right out from underneath you — if you've never felt what it is to be suddenly walking in mid-air with absolutely nothing to stop the fall, if you've never had the experience of discovering that your entire world wasn't there where you thought it was, then you will walk differently. Won't you? Can twenty years do that? Can you, in the space of twenty years, invent a whole new way of walking?

Rita contemplates this question as she stands in the driveway watching her son leave, as if the evolution of this way of walking were a biological marvel. Carrying his white pants, his white shirt, his white socks and sandshoes in his school bag (also containing the lunch she packed for him the previous evening) which is flung over his shoulder, her son is leaving to play cricket. Earlier than usual, and with no explanation, which gets Rita thinking.

His strides are long, his departure rapid, and she can tell that he can't wait to be rid of the street, and not just the street — the house, them, the whole suburb. Everything. She can also tell — and it's not only the fact that he doesn't look back — that he has already forgotten she's there. She may as well go back inside, but she doesn't. There's the nagging thought that he might look back. And if he does she wants to be there to meet that backward glance with a wave. It's this thought that keeps her where she is, that he might just glance back over his shoulder and she won't be there. If she goes inside, she'll never know and the thought that he might have turned to her and she wasn't there will nag at her all day. So she waits. And, of course, he doesn't. The wave she had ready isn't needed.

When he peels off at the top of the street, when he's gone and his bobbing green school bag is no longer there, she swings back to the house — a glittering white house under the Saturday-morning sun — and she knows that one day, sooner more than later, he really will be gone. Everything in his manner, in his speech, tells her this. And the walk. For it is not a walk that is wary of the future. It is a walk that can't wait to get there.

Why doesn't she come inside? Every time it's like this. She stands by the gate and watches the street until there's nothing left to watch. Every Saturday she stands by the gate with her hands in her pockets and watches him get smaller and smaller until he's not there any more. Vic stands by the lounge-room window and watches Rita. Michael doesn't need her to be standing there to get where he's going. He hasn't needed any of them for a long time. But still, she stands there.

It's all that weight. She's shifted all that weight. He could call it love. But he doesn't, he calls it weight. She's shifted it all. From Vic, to the boy. And he feels it, you can tell, the weight of his mother's love. He knows she's got nowhere else to put it now and so it all rests on him. But he shrugs it off because he knows he's going. In his mind, he's already gone. You can tell that too. He's had enough of the old man, the old lady, the house and the whole bloody suburb. Two or three years. Two or three years will go in no time. Unless you're him, of course. Two or three years is an eternity then. But not to her. She holds onto every moment. And she shifts all that weight of hers hoping that it might keep him here a little longer. But she no sooner puts it on him than he shrugs it off. Not that he doesn't want it. It's just that he can't take it with him. Not where he's going, out there into the great world, chasing life. That's why he doesn't turn around and that's why he never will.

Vic turns away from the window. He can will her to let it be as much as he wants, but it won't make any difference. So he walks back to the kitchen where the radio is playing an old song, the way it always does when Vic is in the house. As he enters the kitchen a brief laugh erupts from him like a snort. Was it yesterday? Or the day before? Or last week? It was one of those days they laughed together, Vic and Michael. When the time came, Vic told him — and it would. When the time came to shoot through, he was going to have a bugger of a job getting out of the place. He'd laughed, and Michael had laughed. But not for long because they both knew it wasn't a laughing matter. Not really. They laughed, but in their eyes they were frightened.

It's always like this. She's always watching them walk away. Papa, his trail of pipe smoke floating briefly on the still, autumn air on the day he stepped out of the house and never stepped back in again. Vic with his golf buggy behind him, happy to be off. Vic, always happiest when he's off somewhere. Michael, bouncing into that future that he can't wait to get at. It's always the same. She's always watching them walk away, the men in her life. And it seems as though she's spent her whole bloody life standing at some gate or other, watching them go, and waiting, waiting for them to turn — just once — and wave, so that she can wave back and her heart will be lighter knowing that they cared enough to turn. But until they do her love will be heavy — she knows — and they will all feel the weight of her love when all the time she only wants her love to be light, so she can let it rest upon them without feeling that she is crushing them.

But to do that they've got to turn, and they won't. So Rita walks back to the house, her legs and feet heavy in the newly carpeted hall.

Later that morning while he is waiting for the time to leave so he can step out onto the fairways of the golf course, and while Rita has slipped out for a chat with their neighbour, the nurse in the house behind them, Vic has the house to himself. His mother is sleeping and places no demands on him. He is alone.

He is not a person much given to looking back. But this morning, wandering about the yard —

watering the plants that he swears sing to him when he does — he sees only the past wherever he looks. These moods come upon him and shut down the summer sun when they do. This morning it is more like a spell, one that he can't shake off. And wherever he looks he does not see the new coats of paint, the new plants, the new room added to the house which is now Michael's bedroom. He sees none of this. Wherever he looks he sees only signs of the old life. When he glances up the side way he doesn't see the new path of crushed rock; he sees it when it was dirt and weeds, and remembers Michael playing one bright, innocent morning with his tin and plastic trucks, utterly absorbed in his world, chatting to himself, oblivious to everybody around him. It occurs to Vic that possibly even then Michael had reached the point where he didn't need them any more. And, at the same time, he poses himself the inevitable question. What happened to it all? It is precisely the kind of looking back that he never allows himself. But today it won't go away. There is no reason for it, except that he is alone in the house, apart from the sleeping figure of his mother, who sleeps more and more now, eats less and less, and whose eyes have an increasingly bewildered and lost look about them. Whatever the reason, this morning it won't go away, this nagging question of what happened to it all. And what was he doing when it was all slipping away? Why wasn't he looking more closely? Because, he now knows, it will never happen again — not this combination of people, time and place. They were a species unto themselves. Perhaps not a very happy one, but a species.

A few moments later, in the house, a song is playing on the plastic radio by the fridge. Although he loathes this song, its cheap feelings and cheap strings, he stays, nonetheless, seated in the kitchen, in its thrall. What he doesn't know, at this moment, is that he will hear this song again one morning in the few years left to him, in the small one-bedroom flat he will rent, in the small harbour town with which he associates freedom (a postcard of which is currently stored in his socks and handkerchiefs drawer). The song will ruin this morning that he has not yet lived, as well as the afternoon and evening that will follow it. He will be plagued by the past. It will sit on his back and be with him throughout the carefree day. He will remember the sadness that fills this bright, Saturday-morning kitchen, and that very same sadness will return to him when this cheap song comes back into his life via the radio. He will be annoyed and angry with himself in that morning yet to be lived, because he will know in his heart of hearts (for which his pills will be utterly useless by then) that there is nothing cheaper than being moved by a cliché. Yet he will have been, just as he is now. For this song, this harmless, airy thing that is currently filling the kitchen with its silliness, will bring with it the baggage of all his pasts, presents and futures, and what he calls freedom will be just another town after all.

26

Inside St Catherine's

There is nowhere to go. There is never anywhere to go. She lives in the Home, he cannot enter the place and nor can he invite her back to his home. It is not the sort of home he could invite Kathleen Marsden to, for the very nature of the place and all the things that had happened inside it over the years make it impossible. They would have to wait for different days and different houses.

There is nowhere to go and he has come to this primary school on a brilliant Saturday morning to watch her play. No one, she tells him, has ever come to watch her. So he sits and observes her from a bench near a primary school playing field. And she is good. He can see that at a glance. Very good. Like a grown-up among children. She is good at this game that is a kind of baseball, the name of which he always forgets. Her body — which is now different from the shy body that gets about the schoolyard — is fast, and decisive when she moves. But most of all she has that rare thing, anticipation. He is aware he is watching a different Kathleen. He can't believe she needs to be told she is good, but if nobody from the Home comes to watch her, then it is possible she has *never* been told. He resolves to tell her.

There is less of her that is unknown to him, this girl who has never known her parents and feels no loss. She is, she has told him — carefully pronouncing the official words for her situation — a ward of the state under the care of the Mission of St James and St John. She pronounces the names 'St James' and 'St John' as if they were personal guardians who stopped at the Home often and looked in on her. Once, during their walks to and from school, he dared to ask her the one question that is always on his mind — what is it like?

'If you've never had something, you don't miss it.' Experience had made her practical. 'I don't think about it.'

And that was that. They could have talked more because she didn't mind. It wasn't, as he'd imagined, some deep, awful thing that she was reluctant to bring up. No — the tone of her voice, the look on her face insisted — experience had made her practical. But even as he nodded in quiet understanding, he didn't believe it. When she asked him to come and watch her play, he said nothing. Only nodded twice. Yes, I can. Yes, I will.

So he sits and watches. Occasionally she looks about and catches his eye. Experience may have made her practical, but when everything stops — and the side that was fielding becomes the side that is batting — a quick smile passes across her face, the sort of smile that delights in the knowledge that, at last, there really is someone out there after all. It's the kind of smile that may well have been locked up inside her throughout a whole adolescence of sunny, Saturday mornings, but which would have been impractical to release until now.

Only when she is finished and he is telling her (as he resolved to do) that she is good, like an adult among children, only then does Kathleen Marsden tell Michael that the entire Home has gone to the beach and she can show him where she lives. Would he like that? Can he come? And he gives her two nods again. Yes, he would. Yes, he can.

The wide sweeping lawns, the wide circular driveway, the deep green of the shrubbery, the tall shady trees and the wide open sky — there is no suburb here, only what might have been twenty, thirty, forty or fifty years before the suburb ever came. There is no sign of anybody, except for Kathleen Marsden and Michael. Kathleen's eyes dart quickly about the grounds, to the windows and doorway of the Home itself, looking for signs of unexpected life as she leads Michael up the gravel driveway.

The roses on stakes are in bloom, the shrubs along the driveway are not disturbed by any breeze, and the air is Saturday-morning warm. The summer heat rises from the ground in visible waves, and the Home shimmers behind the rising heat as if part of another world altogether.

Michael gazes at it in wonder as they pass under the cast-iron pillars that support the balcony and into the shade of the wide verandah which runs all around the house. As they approach the front door Kathleen Marsden turns, her index finger to her lips. He can almost hear the walls of the house breathing, almost hear the soft sound of sheets being folded and put away in cupboards on quiet afternoons long past, the dull thud of pillows being plumped, the distant tinkle of silver cutlery — the soft sounds that houses, withdrawn from the world as this one is, always have. For houses such as this, it seems to Michael, are always filled with the quiet sounds of some other time. While the world around them changes, houses such as this stay still. And, in time, the sounds they make become the sounds of another age. His heart is pumping blood the same way it does when he walks back to his mark to bowl the first ball of a new match, and he too is keenly looking about the grounds of the Home for signs of unexpected life, but there are none. With one finger still at her lips, Kathleen Marsden turns the handle and together they enter the Home.

This, she is saying — a self-conscious touch to her voice that wasn't there a few moments ago — is the dining hall. Once it was a ballroom. Did he know that? When the house was grand, people danced here. As if she were a tour guide, her hand sweeps lightly through the air indicating various items in the room. It is plain for a ballroom, a bit on the dark side and cool. He can't imagine people dancing here. For a moment, her eyes resting on a small vase containing yesterday's daisies, he suspects that she may be ashamed of her home and he feels that he ought to have said something, or perhaps that he oughtn't to be here. Suddenly, the whole thing is awkward. She points to four long dining tables, chairs, religious paintings, and the flag, looking down on everyone from the main wall, and stares at it all (he imagines), like someone seeing everything through two pairs of eyes. She tells him how it all works — the breakfasts, lunches and dinners — and the self-consciousness slowly leaves her as she walks round touching the tables and chairs and she becomes increasingly lost in thought.

The light is dull, it doesn't matter, she is the brightest thing in the room — her skin still hot from sport. Giving up to her brightness, to this light she brings to the room and the dreaminess in her voice, he dwells on her like he has never dared to dwell on her before. Not that she notices. She has drifted to a place at one of the four long tables. Before she speaks he guesses that this is where Kathleen Marsden sits. Once, when she was younger, she sat down there, she says, dreamily pointing to the far end of the dining room where the juniors sit, eyeing her old spot as if the small girl that she once was were still sitting at her place waiting to be dismissed. Now, I sit here. Her hands rest on the chair and she leans lightly against it. Her awkwardness is gone. She is lost in her memories and he can dwell on her as much as he likes. She gives names to all the other chairs — who they are, what they all say, who laughs, who talks, and who hardly says anything at all.

'There,' she says, glancing up and catching that look in his eyes. 'It's just a room, isn't it?'

She nods in the direction of the stairs as she leads him from the dining hall. At the base of the steps she is alert again, looking for signs of unexpected life in the house.

'Quick,' she says, and rushes him up the stairs. For a moment he feels as though she is about to take his hand. Perhaps she was. But she doesn't. Then, on the landing, they lift their eyes and are looking through an open door.

The room is bare and sad and exciting because this is where they sleep, the girls of the Home. Sleeping is a very private matter and he walks slowly about the room careful not to upset anything, observing the white metal beds (like beds in a hospital), the worn linoleum floor, the light through the lace curtains. He walks lightly, as if the girls of the Home were in their beds all around him and he is wary of disturbing their sleep. And all the time Kathleen Marsden is standing in the doorway looking up and down the hallway which is dark on a bright Saturday morning, her face, Michael is convinced, now clearly saying that she must have been mad to ever invite him in.

This, he tells himself, this is where she sleeps. Where her eyes close and open at the ends and beginnings of her days. This is where she brings the things that she never talks about. Michael's room is thick with memories and dreams — the raised voices from years before, the fights long dead, the dream of the perfect ball — and once there they never go away. The room keeps them. To be in the room where Kathleen Marsden sleeps and dreams is enthralling. He walks slowly about, touching the metal bed frames, brushing his fingers across the fine lace curtains where the sun streams in and eyeing the religious portraits on the wall because it is all so mysterious. This is where she comes at the end of each day, where she relaxes her mind and body and where she becomes her dreams. But which bed? There are seven in the room, the mattresses all sagging deeply in the middle from years of sleeping bodies, and he has no idea which is hers. There is nothing to tell him. There are no bedside tables. There is nothing personal anywhere in the room.

Then, as if reading his thoughts again, she leaves the doorway and advances slowly over the smooth, scrubbed surface of the linoleum and stops at the bed next to one of the high windows through which the light streams. She touches the bed frame and says, 'Here.' She is the first to see the light in the mornings, she explains. She can lie in her bed by the window in her corner of the room, pull the blinds back, and be the first to see the light coming through the trees of the old Boys' Home opposite that is now closed. As she talks about it, the dreaminess comes back into her voice and eyes. She forgets all about him and her eyes rest on that corner of the room that is hers and hers alone, but not for much longer (not that Michael knows). This rectangle of space by the window is where she brings her private self, where she succumbs to the very private matter of sleeping. And while she is gazing upon the metal frame of the bed — left over

from when the Home was a military hospital —
while she is oblivious of him and dwelling upon that
corner of the room where she has slept since she
was a girl, a car door slams downstairs and she lifts
her head.

Again, she raises her finger to her lips and they
both turn to the door in anticipation of footsteps on
the stairs, each knowing that there is nowhere to run.
They wait in silence by her bed for the first sound of
footsteps. But there is only their breathing. And she
is bright again. The brightest thing he has ever seen.
She is beside him, inches away, her face still warm
from sport, her hands by her side, only a movement
away, and he contemplates the motion required to
close the gap, the sensation of his hand brushing hers,
and is at the point of making that movement and
bridging their worlds, when the car door downstairs
in the driveway slams once more.

She spins round to the window and is suddenly
gone from him while she watches the fruit and
vegetables van follow the circular drive out onto the
street and back into the ordinary world of the
suburb. But when she turns back to him there is a
smile in her eyes, a curve on her lips. Until she
turned he assumed she had no knowledge of what
almost happened, but now he is not so sure for this
is the smile that he saw on her face years before
when they were children, the same smile that was

not meant for him then, but which now is. And somewhere in that smile she knows his thoughts, and although nothing came to pass, he feels for all the world that he has as good as touched her.

A few moments later she leads him along the circular gravel path that the fruit van departed along, keeping close to the shrubbery and trees so that no one will see them. Saying nothing, periodically raising her finger to her lips. Even on the footpath she is wary of the world.

'Well,' she says and folds her hands in front of her as she speaks. 'Now you know.'

Then there is that smile again and she is gone, back into the cool dark house. Brighter than the Saturday-morning sun.

27.

Driving to the Match

An hour later, while Rita is sitting in the house looking out the lounge-room window, Vic is on the fairway, and Kathleen Marsden is in a shaded corner of the Home gardens, Michael is in an overcrowded car driving to the match. He is nauseous. The drive always brings him to the point of vomiting. It's not just the sweet smell of chewing gum, the hot plastic seats and the car exhaust. Five passengers are crowded into the tiny Morris Minor. Apart from the driver — a young churchmember who organises Sunday Bible classes — everyone is in their cricket whites, their bags and bats on their knees. Michael sits next to the rear window, his head half hanging out, the breeze fanning his face.

They are driving to a large park next to a river.

Old trees line the boundary that runs alongside of the river and there is shade under those trees. It is a ground he enjoys playing on, green and even, the way grounds in all the cricket books are — not the dusty paddocks he is used to. On such grounds he can imagine cricket being played as they play it in books and on television. Trees shade the boundary, the field is mown regularly and the lawnmower leaves circles of pleasant green where it has been, the whole ground ringed with shades of green, radiating from the centre to the boundaries like the rings of a tree trunk. The approach to the wicket is even and smooth and Michael knows he will be able to bowl without the fear of falling over in potholes.

With his head half out of the window and the breeze on his face, Michael thinks of the ground to which they are travelling and the more he thinks of it the less he notices the sweet, sickly scent of the chewing gum that fills every corner of the car despite the windows being down. The more he thinks of the ground the less he notices the hot plastic seats, the occasional exhaust belched up from beneath the car, and the less he hears the talk around him and the motion of chewing jaws.

But in spite of all this he is soon listening to the driver — the young man who organises Sunday Bible classes, whose nose is small and pointed and whose hair is smooth and flattened with oil.

Michael is listening because he heard the word 'Russia'. The driver is talking about fences. They have, he says, barbed-wire fences to keep the people in. And as the houses and nature strips and lawns pass by in a blur, the driver continues to talk of barbed-wire fences because these are the types of fences found in Russia. Everybody in Russia wants to leave but they are stopped by these fences. The car is silent, everybody's jaws have ceased their relentless chewing, everybody is listening to this talk of fences and barbed wire.

'I don't know if it's that bad,' Michael says almost to himself as he looks out the window. But he isn't, he is speaking to the car — or, more accurately, to the driver. As soon as he speaks, a different kind of silence settles over the car. It is different from the attentive silence that filled the car when the driver was speaking — that silence was similar to the silence of Sunday classes, when this young man talked about the New and Old Testaments, lessons Michael never listens to because he only wants to play cricket. The silence that fills the car after Michael has spoken is the sort of silence that follows when somebody has said the wrong thing, when people realise that although someone may be one of their number, they are not one of them. It is a silence that excludes him. After a long, thoughtful pause, the driver speaks.

'So, you don't think it's that bad?'

'No.'

He doesn't really know if it is that bad or not, but the driver drags the comment from him and Michael will gladly say it again just to see his nose betray the most minute of twitches.

There is no other response from him though, and they drive on in silence to the ground where old trees line the boundary and provide shade. This second silence lasts the whole way to the ground. This second silence, Michael notes as block by block, brick and weatherboard houses clatter by, completes his banishment.

He is content to be banished. Banishment is fine. They talk a lot at the club about playing for the team. But Michael has never played for the team. He has no time for teams. His cricket is personal. He has never told anybody that every time he steps out on the field he plays for himself and not the team because it is not the done thing. He plays *in* a team because he has to in order to play at all, but he has never played for a team. He is a bowler, and bowlers — he is convinced — go it alone. And so, Michael plays for himself — and for speed. For it is speed and speed alone that will one day lift him out of his street, his suburb and this whole sickly world of chewing gum and plastic seats.

Larwood played for his team and look what they did to him. Only mugs played for the team. He wants to talk further about this, but keeps his thoughts to himself as the car approaches the ground, and the dark, cool shadows of the trees that line the boundary come into view.

28.

The Lesson of Harold Larwood

That night Michael is sitting in his room at the small student desk his father polished and varnished for him one Sunday the previous autumn. As his father watched the desk dry in the midday sun he told Michael that he now had a place to work, that it was important that he should have a place to work, and that this was it. He was very definite about that and watched with satisfaction later that evening when Michael arranged his books on the shelf and his mother took a photograph. The scholar at work, his father said and his parents laughed. He knew that he should have joined in and laughed with them, but the time for all that was gone. He was sixteen and he just wanted them out of his room, and his face told them he wanted them out — and so they left.

Now, the day's cricket completed, he is sitting at the desk and where there would normally be school work there are books on cricket. It's late, the house is sleeping. He has the lamp on beside him and he is reading. He is lost in the world of Harold Larwood. The very name — Larwood — is spoken by everybody he knows in the same way that people speak of a famous criminal. A thug. A gangland hitman who liked his job a little bit too much, and did it a little bit too well. This is the Larwood that Michael has grown up with. A name. Someone who may or may not have lived — a long time ago — but not someone who could still be living. A name, like Billy the Kid or Al Capone. A gangland cricketer. And one that Michael should hate. Instead, he is enthralled with Larwood's world. Photographs of Larwood in action are spread across the desk, newsreel stills that break his action down to its various stages — the long approach to the wicket, low and swooping, almost as if he were in flight, like an eagle flying low, just above the ground, smooth and straight, swooping in on its prey — all finishing in the famous thump of his left boot on the pitch, and the smoothest delivery stride imaginable.

Nowhere is there any sign of pain. Pain must be there. But you can't see it. Pain is not something that can be pictured, it can only be spoken of. And even when it is spoken of it cannot be felt, unless the pain is yours. The pain that Michael is sure is there belongs to Larwood. But the picture before Michael on the desk only shows him the perfection, not the pain. In the jumping black-and-white footage of his imagination, Michael sees a batsman walking out to the centre of the Melbourne Cricket Ground a long time ago in the days of Larwood. Michael has forgotten the batsman's name, but he has read what he had to say about this walk, which was very long and very frightening. Frightening because this batsman, whose name he can't remember, is walking out to face the incomparable Larwood for the first — and, as it turns out, last — time. He stands at the non-playing end of the pitch and waits for the bowler. He does not look at Larwood as he approaches the wicket because he does not want to, and so he stares at the batsman at the other end of the pitch and sees the fear in his eyes. The batsman at the other end is not a man who normally plays with fear in his eyes, but fear is unmistakably there at that moment. It is apparent to everyone — the batsmen, the fielders, the bowler. It occurs to him, this batsman who has just walked to the middle of the Melbourne Cricket Ground, that he has never known the smell of fear, but he is exuding fear now and is convinced that everybody can smell it. And just when he thinks that Larwood will never arrive, that the ball will never be bowled, and that this interminable moment will never be seen through, there is a sound like the sky has been torn open. A rasping, scraping thunder. And this batsman cannot place the sound, for it is sudden and seems to be all around him in an instant. Without being aware of it, his eyes have followed his ears and he is looking down at the pitch and he realises that this rasping thunder is the front foot of Harold Larwood landing on the MCG pitch. Michael tries to imagine the front foot thunder of Harold Larwood, but can't, for it is the messenger of unimaginable speed. There must be pain in the feet and back of such a bowler, but the pain is not apparent in the photographs before him. Nor is the sound. What he sees is a silent, still study in perfection. The series of newsreel images chart the progress of Larwood's foot slamming into the pitch. This is where the thunder comes from, for the tearing sound that this batsman finds so incomprehensible is Larwood's front foot scraping the ground as his body continues on without any visible sign of slowing down.

Here is the thing that Michael still can't understand, and possibly never will. When Larwood's front foot stretches out, when his arm rolls over and the ball is released, and even when he follows through — he doesn't slow down. When he lets the ball go he is moving at the same pace he was during his run. The photographs show no sign of slowing. Michael studies the stills again and again, for he knows that this is the moment, the one that matters above all others — because this is his gift. This is where his speed is. Harold Larwood was a mole in the Nottingham coalmines where he worked, and a kestrel above them. He was blessed with the gift of speed, and with the ball in his hand the mole became a kestrel. You can't hate something that perfect. The more Michael studies the stills in front of him, the more he appreciates that this is what it means to have the gift of speed. But as much as he studies the stills, as much as he isolates the moment that is Larwood's gift, he still can't understand how it's done. And neither, he suspects, does Larwood himself. He would simply say that he just runs in and lets the ball go. That he gets in there and has a good try and does the best he can. That it's for others to talk about it, for when you're perfect you don't have to talk — your action talks for you. But Larwood, the mole who shed his darkness, and who soared up into the daylight utterly transformed by his gift, had one fault. He played for the team. And look what it did for him.

There is a story on the desk in front of him. Michael has read it a number of times because it contains a lesson. It is 1948. Larwood is sitting in the back room of his mixed business in Blackpool. The name Larwood is nowhere to be seen in the shop — at the front or inside. The name Larwood doesn't exist. He sits, a little man, talking quietly, sniffing snuff, chatting to someone he once played against — the man who is telling the story. And although the room is covered with photographs of his playing days, he wants to forget it all.

In the story they talk about the old days, about old friends and places they shared. But nobody talks of the events that made the name Larwood what it is — or the word, 'Bodyline', that is forever part of those events. There are words — not many — that don't need to explain themselves. Words that *are* their own story. Complete miniatures. Words such as Somme and Larwood. And just as nobody mentions the events that made Larwood such a word, nobody mentions the word that accompanies him wherever he goes. These names do not arise in the quiet conversation that takes place at the back of the shop as the snuff is passed around and the tea is poured, just as the name Larwood does not appear in the shop.

He is sad, this Larwood. There are times in the story when Michael expects him to rise from his seat, fling his snuff to the floor, and shatter the quietness of the room with everything that he has kept inside all the years. Times when Michael wants him to rise and shout — 'Apologise! I could play again if I apologised! Well I wouldn't and I won't! So there you are. I've got nothing to apologise for!' He would then collapse into his chair, resume his customary quiet manner, and pick his snuff up from the floor.

But he doesn't do any of this. No, they sit and quietly talk of the times that brought them all together, and the fact that he didn't play again because he wouldn't apologise is never mentioned. That turbulent time has passed. The world outside has put the whole unfortunate business behind it. And to do that they turned Harold Larwood into a nobody. This miner from Nottingham would have lived and died without raising too many eyebrows had he not been blessed with speed. And that gift should have lifted him into a dazzling, new world of light. He had the gift of speed, but he had one fault. He played for the team. And this, in the end, is the lesson of Harold Larwood. You are playing for yourself. You are always playing for yourself — because the 'team' isn't your team, it's theirs. And they'll drop you the first chance they get. In the end they threw him away — the 'team' — and turned him into a quiet nobody at the back of a shop.

Michael places his cricket books on the shelves at the side of the desk, then gazes upon the shadowy branches of the fruit trees in the yard — motionless in the still, summer air. All around him the houses, the street, the suburb itself, are quiet. The children who play their games in the street are sleeping. The girls who gather outside Younger's house to talk in whispers about boys have gone to their beds. So too have the boys who stand near listening to their talk. The games have gone from the street and the whispers have stopped.

With his books, his magazines and news-cuttings, Michael lives in a world outside this one. He puts his scrapbook to one side of the desk and folds this world away for the night. But he knows it is there, this world. And if he is ever in any doubt that it exists, he has only to open his folders and it tumbles out to meet him.

It is a hot night and he cannot yet sleep. When he is done with the desk he slides his bedroom door open and ambles into the kitchen where he nods to a nurse — their neighbour who is in the house often now, keeping an eye on his grandmother. His grandmother who lies in the room that was once his, day and night, sleeping through the heat.

29.

Webster at Home

The photographs on the mantelpiece of the study display, in a series of cameo portraits, the young Webster — from the teenager standing behind the counter of his father's mixed business, to the Webster of his late twenties, standing on the floor of his first factory. In all these photographs it is the passion in his eyes that he notices.

These are the eyes of a man who not only knew how his machines functioned, but often worked on them when something wasn't right, or hammered some vital cog back into shape, when, from time to time, one of his great metal-pressing machines ceased to function. These were the moments he relished most of all, when he stepped from his office, removed his coat and tie, took up the hammer and set about fixing some faulty machine. He relished not only the labour and the easy transition from office to the factory floor, he also relished the effect it created — for Webster is a large man, broad across the shoulders and an impressive sight with a hammer in his hand. So when he strode from his office and hammered recalcitrant machines back into shape, he knew it was a spectacle. He knew he was creating a stir, and knew that the eyes of the factory, from the floor to the office staff, were upon him. It was at moments such as these that he knew he not only had the respect of his staff, but their admiration as well, and underlying all that was the touch of fear that a good factory needed. When the job was done he would put down the hammer, pick up his coat and tie, and return to his office.

That was when the passion was in his eyes. But on this hot Saturday night, while Michael flicks through his scrapbooks and Vic and Rita sleep, he recalls it only as a cheap stunt, the sort of thing that young lions, like the young Webster, do. Now the memory of such occasions is embarrassing. The sort of stunt that he might have imagined laughing about in the years to come. But, in the end, the sort of cheap stunt that was embarrassing to recall. That was when the passion was in his eyes, and in the places where the camera couldn't go, such as the heart and belly and bowels. That, he notes, is the kind of passion that builds a life's work, the work that defines someone. When you are in the grip of a passion like that, Webster reflects, you do good things and stupid things. But now he doesn't know what to do with himself.

'You're sure you're not coming?'

His wife is leaning in the doorway of the study, a light summer scarf in her hands. There is a movie at the local scout hall that doubles as a picture theatre. His wife is meeting friends there, the wives of local councillors whom she calls friends. It's a warm night and she has decided to walk. They could walk together. He has forgotten all about it, but, in any case, he said no to the idea earlier that day. Now Webster shakes his head again, but he accompanies his wife along the curved gravel path that leads to the front gate. The trees that line the avenue — it is one of the few grandly named streets that lives up to its name — have all grown in the years since they came to the place. The heavy branches of the plane trees, thick with leaves and cicadas, form a canopy over the street. His wife waves as she turns at the corner. The rattle of a suburban train comes and goes. His wife of twenty-three years passes out of sight and he is alone on the street.

As he looks back up the winding gravel path to his house among the shrubs and trees, he is aware that it is back — that this feeling is upon him again. This feeling that leaves him with neither energy nor passion. He runs his fingers through plants that he can't put names to, as he walks back to the house. Does everybody else see it? Surely this look of having neither energy nor passion must be in his eyes as clearly as it was when he possessed them. For the first time tonight he thought he saw something quizzical in his wife's gaze, as if she were on the brink of asking if he were all right. It's not a thing she's had to ask all that often in the past because he has always been a man of passion and energy, and she has always admired that in him. As much as he might have kept his secret from her and everyone else over the last few years, perhaps it is now visible in his eyes.

He pauses midway along the driveway, contemplates the anonymous-looking gardener's shed in a far corner of the grounds and checks the time as he jangles the keys in his pocket.

30.

The Stain Spreads

Do I have too much time, lying here day in day out, with my hip aching so much at nights I can't sleep, and this cold so bad, that, like all summer colds, it just won't go? Too much time to lie here and think. Is that it? Is that the problem? Heaven knows — wherever that is, because I can't take these silly words like heaven seriously any more, and I haven't for a long time — but all the same, heaven only knows, I've always *done* things. Keep on the move, old girl. Keep on the move, I've always said. Because once you stop moving, you'll only start thinking, then you'll only start brooding, and that will be the end of you. Mind you, some people can move and brood at the same time. Vic, for a start. He's a brooder. He wasn't always one, but he is now. And his brooding can fill a whole house. On a bright, clear day he can shut the sun out with his brooding. Just as he can light it up with that big laugh of his, when he wants to.

At least I can get about a bit, even if it is only once a day, and even if it is only to empty this potty under the bed. I hear them talking some nights, I hear the clink of glasses, and I know they're drinking beer and talking, and I know that life is going on out there while I'm lying in here, just as it will when I'm lying somewhere else. When I hear that life is going on out there, I have to go and look, and so I do, with my potty (doily over it, mind you), because I've got to have a reason, haven't I, or else I'm just sticky-beaking — and I look at them all. The whole bunch — Vic, Rita, that boy and all their friends. I look at them and it does me good to see them. Not that Vic can bear me being in the room like that with my potty in my hands. Then they bring me back here, into this room, this bed, and I lie here with nothing to do and no one to talk to and it all starts again — this thinking.

With the thinking comes the feeling that this thing, this stain, just spreads and spreads. That I was wrong when I was young to think that you kept your shame to yourself and when you died your shame died with you and the stain stopped. It doesn't. Like a drop of ink onto a piece of blotting paper, you think it'll just be a little stain, but it never stops, does it? What one, small drop can do! When you think it would have run out and stopped, it's still moving — further and further out from its centre.

I saw it eventually spread into Vic's face when he was a boy and came home with that glum look in his eyes, the look that told me he'd finally worked out the way the world works and discovered that it wasn't fair. I wished I could have gathered this stain up and kept it all with me, but you can't. So this thing passed from me to Vic. I knew it had because I saw it in his eyes. And I see it in that boy's eyes too — the same glum look that comes over his face, the one he wears when he thinks that no one is looking. It's there and he wears it — when he's not banging that bloody cricket ball against that bloody fence. Don't tell me there's not something more than cricket going on there. I've seen him throw the damn thing, I hear it crack against the fence — or what's left of the fence — and I know there's something going on.

Cricket? I've never understood it — with its silly names. As soon as anyone starts to explain the whole damn silly business to me, I stop listening straight away and wait for them to finish. None the wiser and no more interested than I was before. But they don't stop. They go on and on. Even from here, I hear them talking and I hear all those silly words and I know they're all talking about it. And the newspapers, and this little wireless I have beside me here. You can't get away from it. What is it with this cricket? I don't know, I never have known and never will — but when I hear that boy throw that damn thing against the back fence, and I hear the fence giving way to the sheer force of whatever that boy's got in him — I know there's something more than cricket going on. The fact that I don't know what that silly game is all about doesn't matter a bit — because I know there's something going on there that even he doesn't realise yet; something that, at the moment, he can only roll up into a red, leather ball and hurl through the air as fast as he can. Speed. That's all he wants. That's all any of them want. That's something else they can all have on their own because the faster you go through life, the faster you wind up in a room like this with nothing much to do but sit around and think.

If I only had things to do like I've always had I wouldn't be lying round here day after day with this feeling that the stain doesn't stop with me. That nothing stops with you. That even when I'm gone, this thing goes on and on. One drop, and even though you'd think it wouldn't go far, it keeps spreading. If I could only have gathered it all up and kept it with me so that it died when I died, I would have done it. But it's in the house, in Vic's eyes, in the eyes of my little angel who brings me the foaming beers that soothe this cold, and in the eyes of that boy who only knows enough to roll it all up — this thing — into a red, leather ball and fling it through the air with enough speed to crack fence palings and drive us all mad.

In the dark room that was once his bedroom, his grandmother is sleeping through this hot, clammy Saturday evening, her mind going wherever it goes, if it goes anywhere at all. You can shut the night out, but you can't shut the heat out. Yet in the dark of that room, which was once his and which now smells of death, she sleeps and sleeps through the stinking heat, her mind God knows where. Raking over God knows what.

Michael's neighbour, a nurse from the house behind theirs, is sitting at the kitchen table reading a magazine while Michael wanders from room to room. His parents, worn out from looking after his grandmother, have gone to bed. Their door is shut. On the mantelpiece in the lounge room is a photograph of his father on some unknown, long forgotten golf course. He is young, but he looks old to Michael, the way his father and his friends always look old in these photographs, as if they were never young. He is, Michael reflects, a teenager. But the word is all wrong for the photograph, and for the face of the young man casually leaning on his putter. It is a word for another age, a word that carries with it all the songs and fashions that hadn't been invented when the photograph was taken. This word, 'teenager', is waiting for another time, another generation, one that will wear the word with the same ease that it will wear blue jeans and dark glasses.

As he stares at the shot he catches a glimpse of something he never has before; that it is not so much the golf that his father loves, as the space, the openness and the freedom that comes with a buggy and a set of clubs. Perhaps he only ever loved engines in the same way. Not the art of driving, the tricks or the intricacies of the trade, but for the moment when he stuck his head out the window and breathed it all in. All that space.

This photograph is his father in his former life, before his mother, before him. He knows his father had a life before him, that he once walked the world without a thought for Michael because Michael hadn't been imagined, let alone been born. He knows all this, it is no surprise. But he has never stopped and properly contemplated this photograph or any of the other photographs that freeze his father and suspend him in this previous state. Now, he is. And it comes as a shock to realise that this figure, this casual golfer on the distant green of his youth, is only a few years older than

Michael is at the moment. Perhaps, only one or two. The fact that his father had a life before is of no surprise, that he may, in this photograph, be the same age as Michael, is. Time. It is all about time. In front of him is a photograph of a young man leaning on a golf club in such a way that suggests he has all the time in the world, because this is what he assumes. Speed can not only measure the time it takes a cricket ball to get from one end of a cricket pitch to the other, but also the time it takes for a quick snap of a pleasant day on the golf course to become sufficiently distant for a whole new vocabulary — one that includes words such as 'teenager' and 'shades' — to have evolved. The more Michael looks at the photograph the more he becomes convinced that he hasn't got a minute to lose, or time and speed will one day leave him staring at a photograph of himself, standing on some dusty cricket ground wondering where all the years went.

The door to his old bedroom opens and the pale figure of his grandmother is standing in the hallway. She has the look of the lost and bewildered. One who doesn't know where on earth she is. Not, that is, until she catches sight of Michael through the doorway of the lounge room, and a look of recognition passes over her face with a smile; a sense of familiarity comes to her eyes that wasn't there before, and the lost and bewildered look is suddenly gone. As the look leaves her the thought crosses Michael's mind that she's not staring at him at all. That, in this world that only she inhabits now, she is staring at his father on the distant green of his youth and she too is young again, the mother of a boy, once again back in the days when the biological inevitability of this half-world she now inhabits was part of the distant future. For a moment she is herself as she was then, and he, Michael, *is* his father.

It is then that this woman from the house behind theirs, this nurse who has been in the house more and more lately, rises swiftly from the kitchen table and speaks quietly to the pale, thin figure of his grandmother. Their neighbour leads her through the kitchen to the back of the house, and as she does, the white head of his grandmother turns and smiles at Michael.

In his room, Michael stacks his books, folders and clippings carefully on top of the desk. The stories of speed they contain are folded away, and he is finally ready for sleep. He hears the nurse leaving through the back door, this woman called Dot from the house behind theirs. Then everything goes quiet and the house slips into sleep. It has been a long Saturday. He is tired at last. With his eyes shut, he sleeps for the waking day.

31.

Frank Worrell and the Long-Legged Fly of Thought

A little over a hundred miles to the west of the suburb in the old gold town of Ballarat, Frank Worrell is alone in his hotel room. His team has just completed a country game, a pleasant jaunt. The night is hot, hotter than the suburbs. His players are either asleep or quietly drinking downstairs. He hears nothing. His hand is under his head and his eyes are fixed on the window in front of him as the lights of the town, one by one, are soaked up by the country darkness.

On the table is the selected poetry of WB Yeats. It is not his copy. The book was given to him before he left for this tour by a silver-haired, elder statesman from Trinidad; one of those who had fought long and hard to deliver the captaincy to Worrell. Worrell is Barbados born. The islands of his West Indies are scattered. It is cricket that draws them together. Cricket that prompts someone to reach across the islands, across the waters, with the gift of a book. It's a game, of course, but this summer they have been playing more than cricket. This summer nothing could go wrong, which is why Frank Worrell has been alone all summer and why he will remain alone until it finishes. It has fallen to him to ensure that nothing goes astray, that events do not turn bad. He must not only be as good as those who have gone before him, he must be better. It was with a puzzling wink in his eye that this elder statesman from Trinidad gave Worrell the gift of his book. When he first looked into it the book fell open at the poem that has been his companion throughout the summer. And from the moment Worrell opened the book he understood the wink, for there was a marker on its page. It is the place he goes back to on nights such as this, when he cannot sleep. Even though he has read the poem so often now that he has committed it to memory, he has, over the summer, found reassurance in reading it on the page.

It is an old book, one that has been lovingly read over the years. Worrell is a writer and a reader, and the point of the poem his benefactor had selected

— to stand him in good stead — is not lost on Worrell. The trick this fly has, of being able to walk on water, is not so miraculous for a fly. It is the surface tension that allows the fly to take its dainty steps across the stream. It is the surface tension that supports it, while the sheer weight and mass of the watery currents swirl beneath it. It is not so miraculous an act for a fly to perform, but to think like a fly walking on water, day after day, night after night, is another matter. One day, when the summer is over and the games are all done, Frank Worrell will relax and he will relinquish the loneliness of his captaincy, and when he does that he will know what it all took from him. He will know what the cost was, for even now he suspects that the cost will be high. That the strength that is required to think in dainty long steps that do not break the surface tension is immense, and, once that strength is spent, it is spent forever. It is a way of getting through what must be got through, and it can only be done once. Just as it is a way of doing things that can only be done alone.

Now, on this hot Saturday night, the summer coming to a close, he is beginning to feel the weight of his loneliness, and for the first time all summer he is beginning to ask himself how long he can sustain this mental trick. He is aware of being tired in a way that he has never been tired before, a tiredness so deep he can't conceive of ever being the same again. When he returns to this book, to this poem, it is the sustaining reassurance of the words on the page that he seeks, the reassurance that the trick, the trance, can be sustained for a few weeks more, until the weight of these days will fall from him and he will know the cost.

His eyes linger on the page. The night is still. The town dark. In the warm, thick night, a passenger train on the last part of its journey rattles down towards the restless suburbs of the city. Frank Worrell closes his book, the book that has given him a place to go when a place to go was needed. He closes it now, perhaps for the last time and prepares for sleep, for the morning, and the trick of thinking in light, long-legged steps.

32.

The Postcard

She's lying back in her bed, in the dark, with her eyes wide open. It's after twelve. No time to be awake. It's always the same lately, waking in the dark and nodding off just when it gets light. And he's always sleeping in the bed next to her. He's good at sleeping. Always has been. He's got the knack. Rita's always been pretty good at it too. But lately she's been lying in the dark for hours with her eyes wide open, listening to him sleeping away while she dredges everything up. Absolutely everything — her mama, her sisters, her papa, her old house, this place, Vic — being young, being old, dying, and wondering where you go then. The way they all get up in the morning and go to bed at night like it goes on forever.

Then she'll find herself looking at Vic, lying back in the bed with that great hooter of his stuck up in the air like a chimney, hairs sticking out like weeds. He thinks I want him to be like everybody else, she's thinking. But that's the last thing I want. I married him because he wasn't like everybody else. Oh, maybe there are times when a touch of everybody else wouldn't be such a bad thing. I ask him to take that old jumper off and put on something smarter, just once — 'cause he has got something smarter and he looks so good in it — and he snorts. It shouldn't be a big thing — but straight away he thinks I want to turn him into Desmond next door. Which is the last thing I want. I said to him one day, 'Let's pick up and go' — when Michael's gone, which won't be long. I really don't know if my heart's in it, but I say it anyway. Just to let him know that I don't want him to be like everybody else. That *I* don't want to be like everybody else. Neither of us does. So I say it, even though my heart's not in it — and he shrugs. What for? What for, he says. We've got everything we want here — by which he means a railway station and a golf course. Even so, part of me is relieved. But the other part is saying, 'Well, what do you want then?'

Then I find this postcard in his drawer. A postcard of a nice little fishing town. I wasn't snooping. I never snoop. His drawers are his business. I was just putting some handkerchiefs away after I'd ironed them, when I saw the postcard. And that wouldn't have bothered me. There was nothing written on it. It wasn't from anybody. It was just a nice postcard, and I liked the look of the place, like he did, I guess. It had the look of a place you could live in. But then I saw a real estate agent's card and I was suddenly more interested in that than the postcard. I stopped what I was doing and stood there catching my breath — because it took me like that. It might mean something, and it might not. So I decided to forget about it and close the drawer with the pressed handkerchiefs inside.

I wake in the dark and start thinking about everything — Mama, Papa, and Vic, who's sleeping away in his bed because he's got the knack. That's when he's not having a turn, and he hasn't for a while. But still, I'm awake in the night again and the postcard comes back to me. It could mean anything, could mean nothing — and probably does. If I were thinking straight that's what I'd say. But I'm not thinking straight, even I can tell that much. And at this hour of the morning, I convince myself that he's up to something.

Rita turns to look at Vic and all she can see at first is that great nose of his. Then his face, in profile, becomes clearer and she wonders where his mind goes when he's sleeping like that. She wonders about those parts of his mind he's never told her about — those thoughts and dreams he's never mentioned. He's a mystery, this Vic. It's probable that nobody knows him better than her, but what, with that postcard, and the real estate agent's commercial card, she's starting to wonder if she really knows him at all. Like there's this other Vic — always has been. And he's up to something.

33.

The Last Train

The last train clatters over the track that leads down into the city. It is a distant sound. A hollow one, for the clatter of the wheels over the rail joints creates the hollow sound that trains make when they are empty. But, empty or full, it is there. The one thing that draws them all together, the one thing that they all hear. The hollow clatter of the last train on this hot Saturday night as it leaves the suburb on its journey to the city yards.

Webster looks up from his garden chair. It is impossible to sleep, he cannot bear being inside, and he has spent the evening contemplating his moonlit garden and the anonymous-looking shed at the far end of the grounds, the keys in his pocket still jangling, a jangling accompaniment to his restlessness.

Michael turns an ear in the direction of the railway line as he places his folders of notes and clippings back on his shelf, the nearness of Kathleen Marsden still with him. Vic's mother, in half-sleep, is aware of this train passing through her restless dreams and interrupting her thoughts; it's a welcome sound, a familiar comfort in this unfamiliar suburban darkness that surrounds her. Kathleen Marsden lies back in her bed, in the room and the Home that she has now secretly shared with Michael and which is now changed, while a bright, yellow moon beams back at her through the curtains. There really is somebody out there, at last, as surely as that train is out there. She has written to him, that afternoon in her corner of the garden, her first love letter, which she keeps in her school bag and will post when the time comes. Rita, watching the profile of the sleeping Vic in the dark, contemplating that postcard and thinking that she feels a bit like that train out there, a hollow sound on a Saturday night; an empty train pulling out of an empty station, but going through the motions all the same because you never know who or what may be waiting down the line. Some part of Vic, in deep sleep, still hears the thing, still receives its sound and knows that it's out there, still registers the thud of wheels on rail joints and concludes that the train is empty. And in his hotel room a hundred miles west of the city, Frank Worrell hears his own train calling, rattling through the country darkness, on the last part of its journey down into the sleepless suburbs. It is a sound that tells him that the journey is almost over, and that soon he will be able to rest.

There they are. All poised on this hot, Saturday night. Poised between waking and sleeping, thinking and doing, coming and going, beginning and ending, while the last train slips out of hearing and they are left to their thoughts and the voices that crowd their heads, poised as they are, between one thing and another.

Part Five

1ST–2ND February 1961

34.

Nat's Barber Shop

A dusty summer breeze floats up the Old Wheat Road as lazy as the day itself. It is late in the afternoon and the breeze floats past Vaughan's Milk Bar on the left, the Presbyterian Church and the Sunday School on the right, slowly lifting the warm green leaves of the young elms in the Sunday School car park and up past the bicycle repair shop, before dividing briefly round the red-and-white lollipop pole at the front of Nat's Barber Shop. The breeze drifts on, up towards the intersection of the two main roads of the suburb, the railway station and the mills, rose and yellow in the afternoon light. Michael enters the barber shop and Nat looks up from a cropped skull and smiles through two rows of peanut teeth before motioning Michael to a seat at the back of the small shop.

There is a photograph of a town somewhere in Italy on the wall not far from the framed certificate that tells everyone that the owner is permitted by law to open a barber shop. This, apparently, is Nat's town, where he grew up before coming to the suburb — although his history has always been a puzzle to Michael because the name Nat doesn't sound Italian. But he is, and that's his town, the town he returns to from time to time, but has no desire to ever live in again. This is his home now, he says. And this is his shop.

At first Michael doesn't hear the transistor radio sitting on top of the glass cabinet containing rows of American hair oils, brushes, combs and small manicuring scissors. But slowly, he notes the excitement in the commentators' voices; he hears familiar names and realises that a game he had long given up as lost was — remarkably — still in progress. It is then that he looks up to the transistor and then on to Nat, whose eyes are no more than a couple of inches away from the top of the customer's skull.

'Are they still in?'

Even to Nat, this is not a question that needs explaining — who the 'they' in the question are, what this mysterious 'in' is, and why the surprise in Michael's voice that they should 'still' be in. No, there is no need to explain any of this. They are talking cricket.

The customer in the chair replies, his lips moving briefly beneath his cropped skull, without taking his eyes off the mirror in front of him. To Nat, cricket is an oddity, something incomprehensibly English, but he listens and he joins in the conversation because it's good business for one thing, and because (and this is the main reason) he likes people. Whatever people like, he likes, because he wants to share their little pleasures. And it shows. This is his gift. He likes people. He has the gift of getting on with everyone around him. It's natural, not forced, not a sales pitch. This is why Nat has the most popular barber shop in the suburb. This, and the fact that he also does a classy cut. The type of cut that — like Rita's dresses — this suburb had never seen until Nat came along.

The close-cropped skull that he is working on belongs to the bicycle repair shop owner. He is a man who doesn't like people. He doesn't even like himself, which might explain things. He is a man without gifts. People come to him merely because they have bicycles in need of repair.

The transistor radio on top of the glass cabinet of Nat's shop brings them all together. The man who likes people, the man who doesn't — and Michael. They are all drawn into the dying minutes of a drama being played out on a hot summer pitch five hundred miles away in Adelaide. They'd had two days of stinkers there, and now the stinkers were heading east towards the suburb because Adelaide weather always does. From his seat in Nat's Barber Shop Michael can imagine the heat rising from the ground the way it always does at the end of a hot day's cricket. Nat stands still, his scissors and comb in his hands, as he stares out through the window at the peach glow of the Old Wheat Road, the deep shadows and the ripe walls of the shops opposite. He has stopped cutting and the bicycle repair shop owner seems to neither notice nor care. He is staring at the shop ceiling. Michael eyes them both, but like them, he is concentrating on the dying minutes of this drama being played out five hundred miles away. What, he wonders, is the barber so struck by that without seeming to be aware of it, he has dropped his arms to his side, scissors and comb still in his hands. It is not the cricket, for by his own admission, he knows nothing of the game. It is — he always says with a shake of the head — a mystery. It occurs to Michael that because he knows nothing of the game, because what the shrill, rising voices of the commentators on the transistor tell him means very little, he can make of the drama what he will. It is the voices of the commentators that he is listening to, the drama in their delivery, not what they are saying. Michael and the bicycle repair shop owner are listening to the dying moments of a dramatic game of cricket. The barber, Michael idly speculates in his vinyl chair at the back of the small shop, might just as easily be listening to the dying moments of a famous opera. The great Hall, the gum-chewing Mackay and the clownish hero, Kline, could all be players on a wooden stage rather than a green field.

Barely aware of having risen, Michael moves towards the seated figure of the bicycle repair shop owner and the standing figure of Nat, as the commentator announces the final over of the day and the game. As he stands beside the two he looks briefly out across the street to where the butcher, the chemist and the newsagent are gathered round the butcher's radio, and he imagines that all along the street, and all across the suburb, everybody is doing exactly the same thing.

The commentators are calm, then shrill, then calm again as they find the words that will become pictures in people's minds. They must find words that correspond with the facts (batsman, bowler, ball, pitch, grass, sky, sun), and when they do, when the facts and the words correspond, pictures are created in the minds of the listeners; pictures that, in the end, will be more lasting and more meaningful than the photographs of the events that Michael will see in the morning newspapers. Years from now when Michael recalls this game, it will be the word-pictures currently being created on the radio that he will remember.

This last over passes slowly because the great Hall is bowling and his walk back to his mark is as long as the late-afternoon shadows Michael imagines falling across the ground. At one point the crowd pours onto the ground because they think the game is finally finished and their tensions can be released. But the game is not finished and they must all go back to their seats as the word 'pandemonium' rises above the crackle and the static. For the second time in six weeks Michael's world and all those in it fall silent and still for the last ball of a cricket match — the ball that will decide if one side has lost or if it is a draw.

And when it is over — when the gum-chewing Mackay has put his body into the line of the ball and felt the thud and sting of it hitting his ribs (because you can't get out hitting the ball with your ribs), when the crowd has spilled onto the ground for the second time in as many minutes — the barber shop, the butcher shop, and all the shops and houses across the suburb, burst into life and the tension that has been curled up inside everyone is suddenly released in a carnival of sound. For a moment, watching the smiles on the faces of everybody near him (smiles that glow with the late-afternoon light), Michael could almost like the bicycle repair shop owner — this man who doesn't like people, who doesn't even like himself, but who has suddenly discovered that he just might like people a little more than he thought. For this is not a victory. It is a draw. Nobody has won, and everybody has. Like the perfect ball that Michael will one day bowl, this is an event. Everybody, for a short time, has been drawn together by this thing, and it seems to Michael that everybody found something inside them that wasn't there at the beginning of the day.

As the bicycle repair shop owner leaves the shop — waving to Michael for the first time in memory — Michael takes his place in the barber's chair and Nat smiles broadly at him through two rows of peanut teeth.

In the nets, as the last of the day's sunshine fades to twilight, there is pain in his back. Some pain is always there. That is to be expected. It is also expected that the pain will go as the day progresses. But as Michael prepares himself for the final training session before the weekend game (his first with the seniors, with grown-ups), the day has progressed but the pain has not passed. He rubs liniment into his back — a football smell, not a cricket smell — and watches the deep-green pines of

Skinner's old farm, and, beyond, in the distance, the white walls and grey slate roof of St Catherine's.

One must always expect a certain amount of pain. The great Lindwall felt pain — that perfect action, the grace, the balance, the liquid smoothness of it all, was performed in pain. The trick is not to notice it, to be so involved in the business of bowling, that the pain that is there at the beginning of the day disappears when the mind is utterly concentrated on the task of propelling a red, leather ball through the air at speed.

But for the first time in memory Michael bowls with pain. For a moment (something he has never contemplated before), Michael thinks about what it would be like to live a life without speed. What would fill his days? For the days would need filling. But this does not occupy his thoughts for long. They are not young thoughts — and Michael is young. He is simply putting himself in the position of someone older and imagining what it must be like to lose the thing that fills your days; and then he sees the image of his father in the laundry at the back of the house, polishing his boots, packing his bag and preparing for the thing that he did best — the very thing that he can't do any more.

As the shadows lengthen across the oval the pain gradually goes. He doesn't note the point at which the pain disappears, but there comes a moment in the training session when he picks up his ball and counts his paces back to the top of his run and realises that the pain is no longer there.

When he paces back to his marker in this endless procession of pacing, running and bowling, when he walks back to his marker to begin the task all over again, he breathes in the scent of the lawn clippings and the pine trees along the boundary, feels the cool evening breeze on his back, and realises that he is happy. He is happy because he is doing what he does best. This task, this pursuit of speed, fills his days and it occurs to Michael that he just might be at his happiest when he is taking the long walk back to the top of his run, when he is preparing himself to run in, to bowl, and to lose himself utterly in the world of action, rhythm and speed.

35.

Tracing the Black Line

As Michael is sitting in Nat's shop listening to the radio, Rita traces the black line of the railway as it wriggles its way along the coast on the map spread out before her, at one moment almost running on the water, at another withdrawing inland, keeping its distance from the shades of blue that represent the Pacific Ocean. On it goes, wriggling up through the neat blue squares of — what do they call them? — longitude and latitude, in and out of named and nameless harbours and coves. They'd have names, of course. But not on the map that Rita is looking at, her index finger tracing the winding course of the railway line as it mimics the coast, then steps back and hugs the foothills of the inland, until it finally passes through a small harbour town on the New South Wales border.

She doesn't have to imagine what the place looks like, she knows from the postcard. It's as pretty as a picture. But not cute. A real town. The sort of town that happy couples go to in their later years when they've done the right thing by nature, when they've fulfilled their biological function — had their children, brought their children up and watched them leave. The sort of town that people go to when they once more become what they were before they ever had children — a couple. To make a new life with what's left of things. It's also the sort of town that unhappy couples go to, in one last, desperate fling at the way things ought to be. Happy and unhappy couples, all putting together the bits and pieces of their lives after having been families. It's that sort of town.

Vic has his eyes on this town. He may even have plans for it — but he's never told Rita. Not for the first time since seeing the postcard, she contemplates the possibility that his plans — if they exist — might not include her. She knows him, and she doesn't know him. There are times when Vic seems like a simple creature, easy to know. And other times when she can't even begin to understand him, when he's a complete mystery and all those simple creature games like the jokes he loves telling — that used to be fun but aren't any more — are just a disguise, a role he plays so that his mind can dwell on other things — like this small town — without being watched too closely.

Part of her says if he wants to go, let him. Good riddance. But the other part says you don't walk away that easily. Not from twenty years. There's always something else to try. Always another way of doing things — isn't there? Besides, Rita's not the sort of person to be left. She'll do the leaving if it has to be done. She would have once and she could again. But being left, that's another thing. She knows women who have been left, and they've all got the same look about them — a scared, tired look — and she's in no hurry to get that look. Besides, there's a large part of her that will always be hopelessly in love with Vic — against all good advice — a part of her that is forever ready to have another crack at things.

Maybe he hasn't got plans at all. Maybe he just liked the place and kept the card the way people do, the way she has from time to time. A memento. Something to go to and stare at when you need to. And why would he leave it lying around if it really meant all that much? It would be like leaving the photograph of some, some tart lying around. Wouldn't it? Some cheap tart he happened to meet some bloody where or other. He just wouldn't do it.

Not if it really meant something. He wouldn't be that open about it — or that stupid. Besides, this isn't a cheap tart of a town. It's a real town. The sort of place where couples go to start their lives all over again.

She no sooner allows that thought to pass than she acknowledges that men and women really do things like that. That people really do leave things like photographs and letters and bus tickets lying all around the place because they just don't think, or don't care — or in some guilty part of them want to be found out anyway.

She rises from her chair beside the bookshelf and ambles about the house. It's late on a Wednesday afternoon. Vic's at the golf course, Michael's at the barber's. Mary is sleeping. The house is hers. It happens, she says, nodding to herself. She thinks about all this while she contemplates the lounge-room window, one part of her becoming excited with the prospect of French windows and curtains and drapes, another part wondering what the point of it all is.

Vic is standing on the tee of the seventh hole. The fairway runs down into a low dip where the creek that once ran through the whole suburb trickles on as it did before the suburb came. The trick is not to land in the drink. Vic should be thinking about this as he prepares to tee off, but he's not. He's thinking about the art of shooting through. It's all in the timing. Like golf. At the right time and place you can shoot through and almost make it look like you've just ducked out for the shopping or a quick round, when, in fact, you've shot through. The right time and place can make it look like that, and the time, Vic senses, isn't far off.

He mightn't give a cracker about dying, as he said one afternoon at Black's surgery, but he does care about making the years he might have left count — for he knows that the end is nearer now than it's ever been before. He carries this sense of the end being near in his buggy with his clubs as he roams the fairways of the golf course. The time for shooting through is almost upon him, and the last of his living will only be done once he has. But right now, it's still there waiting to be grasped, this moment when he will shoot through and make his last charge at being happy enough — before he shoots through forever.

It must be done alone. He knows that. He could stay, and the world will call him a good enough man when he's gone, but he knows only too well that he wouldn't be worth a crumpet to himself or anyone else. That's why Vic's got this little place picked out, up north. Far enough away to almost be another country. Another life, at least. He's got it into his mind that there, and only there, will he be able to see the whole show out the way he imagines it. He doesn't imagine being there with anyone — a woman, a friend. When he thinks of the town he sees the harbour, the sea, the horizon, and knows that he wants to look at it for every day of what remains to him. A solitary figure on a beach. To some people that might be loneliness. To Vic, as he leans over the ball and prepares to give it a big slap, it's freedom. And that's what he likes about this place up north that he's picked out. It's got that kind of promise.

From the sound of the club hitting the ball he knows that it's all wrong. The sound should be crisp and clean, but it's like he's slapped the ball with a wet lettuce. That's what you get, he thinks, as he watches a small splash erupt from the creek. That's what you get for taking your eye off the ball.

36.

The Blessed Years

It's the blessed years I dream of now, the beautiful blessed years, when he was too old to be called a baby and too young to know what was going on and how things worked. I knew those years were blessed when we had them there in front of us, day after day after day, and I knew they'd go, and they went all right — but I still can't believe they did. Now they come back to me in dreams, and every time I close my eyes I pray — not that I pray any more, and God only knows who I pray to — but I pray that when I close my eyes I'll slip back into those dreams because I'm living it all again when I do. And if I have to die, let me die in one of those dreams, when my boy is back, and all the years are blessed again.

I hear them out there, out there in the lounge room, drinking and talking and laughing. I hear them, and I don't. Tonight I have my memories. These are the years that I slip back into, the blessed years. Not the ones that followed when he'd woken up to what was going on and given up his wide laughing eyes for the glum look the schoolyard gives a kid when he discovers that everybody has a mum and a dad. One day he came back with that look on his face because he knew everybody had something he didn't. And that was when he moved from the centre rows of school photographs to the edges.

I watched his face change and there was nothing I could do — and he didn't ask me to do anything. I gave him the photograph, the only one I've got, the only one I ever had — and said here, this man, is your father. His six-year-old head nodded with the seriousness of a boy grown up too soon. A boy whose blessed years were too short. If I could have done anything, I would have — but what could I do? All I could do was show him the photograph. It's a bad photo. Viktor, the man who gave me fifty one-pound notes in a roll that night the cart took me away from his family estate because I was about to become an embarrassing member of the domestic staff. Viktor, who is now gone. That's the boy's name too — without the 'k'. He took that photo away and never spoke of it, and never asked me anything about him again.

Something left him and it never came back. Even when he started hitting the grog a bit more than anybody should — and I'd say you'll kill yourself like that one day, and he'd say I couldn't care less (and he meant it) — I knew that his nature had turned and that he hated this man — his father — who never wanted him. His response was never to ask about him — and he never did after I first told him — just to let me and whatever invisible witnesses that might be present know, that just as this man, his father, had never wanted to know him, he too would never seek to know his father. He never said as much as this, but his manner did, that even if this uniformed stranger — preserved in a silly studio photograph from somewhere in South Melbourne, when the war was too old to want him, and he was too old to go anyway — even if this uniformed stranger were to seek the boy out as they sometimes did, the boy would never forgive him. He learnt how to hate early, this boy of mine, and I saw all this from the moment his face changed and he brought that glum look into the house.

But we'll always have those years when he didn't know a thing, and the smile on his face lit the whole of that dark house of ours. And these are the ones I go back to in dreams now. The years we got for free, the ones we had before he shrugged that private world of ours off his shoulders (like he was always going to) and found out that something was wrong, and that it could never be put right.

37.

The Gift of Kathleen Marsden

'I'm going away. I thought you should know.'

There is an old stable at the back of the Home. It is a relic, a thing left over from other times when Skinner's farm dominated the community. It is neither part of the new technical school nor part of the Home grounds, but seems set in some no-man's land in between them both on the thick khaki grass where cows once grazed. And perhaps because no one really knows whose land it sits on now, or perhaps because nobody could find the energy or a good reason, the thing has never been knocked over.

It is late in the afternoon. A stinker, and the day is at its hottest. The sky, like the enamel of a car that has been too long exposed to the elements, has been bleached by the white sun which lights up the stable through the half-opened door. The papers of the world out there are filled with the exciting news of the cricket the day before, and photographs of the heroic Slasher Mackay, with his bruised chest, are everywhere. But in this stable they have left that world behind them. Kathleen Marsden is leaning against the stairs, still solid, that lead up to the old hayloft. She is in uniform (they both are), and her long summer tunic falls over her like a sack, down below her knees. In her hand she holds a straw hat, the school badge sown into the front of it, and occasionally she fans herself with it. And Michael, whose head rests on the same wooden stairway — but on the other side of Kathleen Marsden — can almost feel the heat coming off her cheeks and forehead, as well as the smell of the lemon-scented soap with which she has washed.

'Did you hear?'

Of course he had, and of course it had registered with him, but he is slow to respond. It is the day, it is the drowsy happiness that runs through him. And he either finds it too hard to shake this drowsiness off or he doesn't want to break the spell they are under by speaking. But he heard all right, and nods when she questions him.

'They sold the Home. We're all going.'

'Where?'

The drowsiness is all but gone now and he is leaning towards her, one of his elbows resting on the step beside him. Still fanning herself with the straw hat, she names a suburb on the other, far side of the city — a suburb that is only faintly familiar to him and may as well be on the other side of the earth.

'I've known for weeks.'

'Oh.'

He wanted to say more than 'Oh' and could hear his voice in the old stable, sounding as flat as if someone had just told him that his tea was cold. Part of him feels compelled to ask why she hasn't told him till now, but another part of him isn't sure that he has the right to be indignant, and so it comes out 'Oh'.

'I should have told you.'

He shrugs. She stops fanning herself, watches his reaction, sums up the shrug and doesn't take offence. It's not that he doesn't care, she knows that by now. He's just not being pushy.

'It's true. I should have.'

'But you didn't.'

She lets out a hot, summer sigh that, under any other circumstances might have been read as boredom, but is anything else but that. She is leaning back against the stairs, her long summer tunic falling over her like a sack. But he can see her. The sack of the school tunic doesn't matter. He can make her out under the sack and she knows he can. He isn't sure how long the silence has gone on, but she picks up the conversation as if the silence doesn't matter anyway — and it doesn't.

'I was putting it off. I thought that if I didn't talk about it or even think about it, that it wouldn't happen. But it will.'

'When?'

'Saturday.'

If he'd stopped to catalogue what he was feeling — and, of course, he wouldn't until much later — he would have been amazed to discover that all of these things were in him. And he might also have wondered if they'd always been there, just waiting to be touched and stirred by the loss of Kathleen Marsden — or if they hadn't existed before her at all, and that she had brought them into existence simply by being the brightest thing he'd ever seen, and then buggering off just when his eyes had got used to the light. Or was it that they were all there, always were, and always are, these feelings that pop up when the floor drops out from under you. It was another record, another set of grooves, but wasn't it still playing the same bloody song it always had? The only thing he knew for sure was that this time he really was annoyed.

'Are you annoyed?'

'No.'

'You can be. I won't mind.'

He swings round, facing her, tapping the stairs lightly with his fingers. Perhaps she wants him to be annoyed. That if he loved her he would be. That this was precisely that point in the conversation where grown people should be fighting. And if he were more mature he would know all this. But he's not.

'I wouldn't blame you.'

The anger drains from him in an instant. She looks up with the hat still in her hand and he knows from the look in her eyes and the tone of her voice that this is not an invitation for him to be annoyed with her or even to be fighting with her. So he takes those few steps that bring him to her because he knows it's all right. And he knows too the significance of this invitation to Kathleen Marsden, of her being here like this with him in this stable, because she is a girl from the Home and there's no shortage of voices in the suburb that will tell you all Home girls are sluts. If she were to be seen like this she would confirm the talk and make it all true. When she looks up and brings her eyes into line with his, it is clear that she brings the knowledge of all this with her too. It is important to her that he knows this, that he acknowledges it before anything happens, and that he sees that she runs the risk of confirming the idle talk of the suburb if she chooses badly. She needs to be assured that her judgment is good and she can trust him. It's all in her look, and, satisfied that the point is made, she nods.

Her lips are warm and taste of orange cordial. Her neck smells faintly of the yellow, lemon-scented soap the grocer in the Old Wheat Road sells. Once they would have hit each other to show their affections. And somewhere, hidden in a corner of the stable, their playground selves may even be watching, wide-eyed and puzzled by the arms and lips and fingertips of their older selves as they explore this mysterious new way of showing their feelings. When their arms encircle each other they each feel the full form and weight of their bodies as they lean against one another — he through the sack of her school tunic, and she through the grey school shirt and the baggy grey trousers of his uniform.

But as mature as these older selves may be, they reach a point in this delirious exchange where neither of them knows what to do next. And so, their arms still encircling each other, they withdraw and Michael watches as Kathleen Marsden runs her tongue over her lips that must surely now taste of him, just as his taste of her orange cordial.

'Better than hitting each other,' she grins.

He grins back. Then she turns to the open door of the stable, to the white sun and the glare of the afternoon and speaks without looking at him.

'Time to go.'

She pulls a face and their arms drop to their sides.

'There'll be a search party out.'

Outside, in the relentless glare of the early February sun, she is furtive again, looking about for peering eyes as she steps through the long, dry grass and back onto the overgrown path that leads to the rear of the Home. They skirt the main building and slip out into the street by the pathway alongside the cottages. On the footpath she relaxes. He gazes down at her lips and she shakes her head.

'Not here.'

She is right. The window eyes of the Home are watching. She is a Home girl.

'You'll write,' she says. 'You must.'

He nods and she promises to give him the address the next day in the schoolyard.

It is Thursday. By Saturday the Home will be empty and the girls will be gone. While he is eyeing the Home she kisses him once more on the lips, quick as a bird, and is away.

'Bye, Kathleen.'

Even as he speaks he knows it is ridiculously formal given the way they now know each other. And it is while he is dwelling on this that she suddenly turns her head as she walks away over the gravel of the circular driveway.

'Kate,' she calls, without stopping, as if tossing a flower over her shoulder for him to catch. Then she turns back to the Home, no longer Kathleen but Kate.

It is, he realises, her gift. She has no money to buy silly cards or whatever things people buy each other, and so she is leaving him the gift of her name. The name she reserves for her friends, which she gives as if tossing a brightly coloured flower over her shoulder.

38.

A Few Words

When Michael leaves Kathleen Marsden, when he sees the last of her disappearing into the Home, he wanders distracted, along the hot afternoon street with the taste of orange cordial still on his lips. It is one of the few streets in the suburb that has kept its old trees, and the footpath and the street are dappled with shade, but it doesn't stop the heat. He finds himself at the training nets in the school behind the home.

At the nets the bicycle repair shop owner is chewing gum like the heroic Slasher Mackay, and Michael is snapped back into the world of speed, quietly wondering if the bicycle repair shop owner has always chewed his gum like this (and Michael has never noticed) or if he has only recently affected it. His whole mouth works on it, the bones of his jaw moving under his skin like that of a cow grinding its cud. He is not looking at Michael as he talks. He is leaning against the metal railing of the oval as the team prepares for training and Michael is aware of being late for the first time in memory. They are preparing for match practice and he is staring out across the dusty ground as the mats are laid over the concrete pitch and systematically hammered down with the kinds of spikes with which you would hammer a tent down. His lower jaw works continually on the gum and it seems to Michael that even when he speaks he is still chewing.

It is, he says, a hot day. But he does not bother with a sentence. The day is, presumably, too hot for sentences. It is simply the key word itself — hot — that he releases from his mouth as he takes his eyes off the oval and squints into the descending light of the sun and the pale blue of the sky. He pauses and dwells on the implications of the heat before going on. Big step, he says, just when Michael thought their conversation was done. Michael is not sure what he means by this and says nothing. This silence — in a conversation of silences — is noted, and the bicycle repair shop owner adds, his jaw working continually on the gum, that the step he has in mind is the one from kids' cricket to grown-up cricket because Michael is playing with grown-ups on Saturday. His opponents will be, he says in two words, nodding at the mats and the players gathered all around, grown men. He then looks Michael up and down — tall, he notes, but nothing there. The question he is clearly asking himself is whether the kid is ready. And Michael, reading the unspoken question in his eyes, is wondering whether his first impression of the bicycle repair shop owner isn't true after all, that this is a man who simply doesn't like people and that this dislike shows in everything he says and does.

Out on the field the last of the spikes are hammered in and the players, in a mixture of whites and street clothes, walk slowly back from the boundary where the club kit has been dropped. The bicycle repair shop owner watches the players depart the dry ground then turns back to Michael, his eyebrows lifting ever so slightly as he does, and releases two final words — soon know — the movement of his jaw untroubled by speech. He is not the captain of the team, but he speaks to Michael as if he were. The captain is the local real estate agent, a round, jolly man who does like people, who, when the team arrives at the club kit, shakes Michael's hand, says welcome, and introduces him to everyone. The bicycle repair shop owner takes no part in the process and nobody expects him to. His eyes are always still with disapproval whenever he looks upon this jolly round man.

As Michael walks to his bag, as he sits to put his white socks, his trousers and his hat on, he sees the opening bowler of the team putting his leather boots on, and he dwells on those boots — the soles, the thick laces, and the solid leather that hugs the bowler's ankles. He laces his sandshoes, still eyeing the boots, while recalling his conversation with the bicycle repair shop owner and counting the total number of words that their conversation consisted of. It is, he calculates, seven words — 'hot', 'big step', 'grown men' and 'soon know'. Seven words, all of them spoken by the bicycle repair shop owner — none by Michael. Five minutes of conversation. This man offers the world words in the same way and in the same spirit that he offers himself.

While he is thinking this the captain approaches him. He has a small, cloth moneybag in his hands. He passes it to Michael saying that everybody has been given one, that they are collecting money for the team, for a new kit, and would he care to take one. Michael looks from the captain to the moneybag and back again. He can hardly tell this man that he has as little time for the team as he does for this whole pancake suburb, so he quietly takes the moneybag and says that he will do his best, and the captain says that is all they can expect of anyone.

When he steps onto the training field his head is filled with what must be done and he forgets all about the moneybag. He will not think of it again until he discovers it at the bottom of his training bag one warm Sunday afternoon in a few weeks' time. When he sees it, he will know reluctantly what he must do, and his collection duties will take him into the driveways and doorways of the suburb and then on into the foreign, private country of Webster's estate.

Part Six

12TH–15TH February 1961

39.

A Private Country

The high sandstone wall runs almost the full length of the block. Native trees that were here before the suburb ever came reach high up in the mid-afternoon sky. The heat is heavy, the birds have given up, and the trees — like the street — are still. Nothing is moving, not even Michael, who stands in the shade of a white gum at the entrance to Webster's mansion. The wide gate, as always, is open. Michael stands in front of it, pauses in thought, peering into that closed world that exists behind the wall — and it is a wall, not a fence — before stepping over the line and entering the grounds that he has only ever glimpsed from the street.

Those glimpses do not prepare him for the first, overwhelming impression of looking at Webster's mansion from the inside — that immediate feeling of being in another country. The grounds are vast. He can see no end to them. Lawns, paths, gardens, wooded sections like small forests, go on and on as far as he can see. He can spot no sign of the three remaining walls, which are either hidden by the foliage or too far away to be observed. And winding through it all, is the wide, sweeping gravel driveway that leads up to the house itself.

He walks slowly, not because of the heat, but because he knows he is out of his territory. He is in another country; these endless lawns, these small forests, these winding paths, all belong to someone's private country. He wouldn't be surprised to come across a railway station somewhere in the gardens — a personal train, and a personal driver just sitting there. Always on call. As he follows the crunching gravel driveway, he nears the house itself. It has two storeys, and is as high and wide as the Girls' Home nearby. As he nears it he can see that everything has been carefully looked after, that the house almost looks a little too clean to be old, the paint too shiny, the iron balcony too sparkling.

The upstairs windows are open to catch whatever breeze the afternoon may bring, but Michael can't see anybody about. Standing before the house he listens hard for sounds of life — a radio, a raised voice, the rattle of a dish, but there is nothing to be heard.

Then, looking about him once more — after closely observing the gardens and lawns and pathways — he leaves the gravel driveway, walks slowly up the stone steps and knocks on the front door. The sound of the large metal knocker disturbs the whole property — if not the whole suburb — and he looks back towards the front gate, suddenly afraid, but not sure of what. As thunderous as that single knock on the front door may have seemed to Michael, it has disturbed nothing. He tries again and there is no response. The house, the garden, the whole property, seems to be deserted.

Michael relaxes, forgets his reason for being there in the first place, and decides to stroll about the property, to explore it as if it were a public park. He leaves the new front steps — that show no sign of wear — and follows a small, winding gravel track that runs off the main driveway. On the vast lawn to his right he sees the first signs of habitation — a mower parked by a low mound of grass, gardener's gloves and a rake. A little further on a wheelbarrow, containing pots ready for planting. Later, as the track takes him still deeper into the mansion grounds, a bench with a sun hat perched upon it. But no sign of anyone. Michael is beginning to wonder if some disaster has taken place without his knowing and the whole suburb is like this — something so sudden that no one had time to pick up their hats and gloves, before hastily departing. The grounds have the ghostly look that things have in dreams, when some inexplicable disaster strikes without warning.

He brushes his hands across some ferns in a shaded patch of the grounds. Above him a few birds warble in response to this disturbance then go quiet again. It is, indeed, another country, another place entirely, this mansion of Webster's, and Michael is at the point of leaving when he sees what he at first takes to be a gardener's shed. But there is something about the way this shed is tucked away, something in its very manner that suggests it doesn't want to be discovered. Curious, he wanders on, intent only on having a quick look before departing. The large, garage-like doors are open to the gardens. There is another wheelbarrow parked next to it, a rake and a tray for the lawn cuttings. He starts as a bird flaps from a shrub close by, and then, as he nears the shed, he hears voices. He doesn't know if he should stay or go, because the voices are hushed and the tone of the conversation is the tone that people adopt when they don't want to be heard. This is a confidential conversation and he doesn't really want to disturb it. But he is only a few feet from the shed door. The path he is standing on is gravel. It is quite possible that if he turned to leave whoever was behind the shed door would hear him depart and his departure would look highly suspicious. So, deciding that he has done nothing wrong, that the front gate to the property was open after all, and that he may as well go forward as go back, he takes those extra few steps that lead him around the shed door to greet the speakers.

The man on his immediate left is tall and broad-shouldered. He is wearing a tie, suit trousers and shiny black shoes. This, Michael knows straight away, is Webster — the same man he saw earlier this summer standing in the doorway at the back of his factory. The other man, wearing overalls and holding a spanner, he doesn't know. At first neither of them even notices him. And Michael barely notices them. All he can see is the gleaming, black nose, the sweeping curves, the smooth chrome trimming of what he knows is a rich man's sports car. Michael doesn't care about cars. You can't bowl a car. Cars simply take you to and from cricket grounds. But there are boys at school who talk about cars all the time — who make drawings of cars in their exercise books when they should be making charts of climatic classification. These boys simply refer to it as an E-type. Consequently, even Michael knows that this is a famous car, famous enough for schoolboys to draw and dream about.

He doesn't know how long he has been staring at the car, but when he looks back to the two men they are eyeing him with a similar expression of astonishment. Webster studies the boy's face and traces his line of vision, from his eyes to the nose of the car and back again. And when Webster meets Michael's eyes, it is clear that they both understand each other perfectly. Webster, Michael knows, has no trouble reading his thoughts and has no trouble identifying the conclusions that this young intruder has reached. Without need of even seeing his own face, Michael knows it is an open book. 'You,' the look on Michael's face says, 'It's you.' And, just as Michael's face is transparent, so too is Webster's. At the same time that Webster is reading Michael's thoughts, Michael is reading his.

Webster orders the man in overalls to throw the tarpaulin back over the car, then turns his attention to Michael.

'Well, good afternoon, young man.'

Michael watches the green canvas shroud fall over the automobile.

'The gate was open,' he says.

'The gate is always open. What can I do for you?'

Michael takes the cloth moneybag from his trouser pocket.

'I'm collecting for my club. We're buying a new kit.'

'Oh. What's wrong with the one you've got?'

'It's old,' Michael says, still distracted. 'And it's

falling apart,' he adds, eyeing the man in the overalls who says nothing.

'Well,' says Webster, breaking into a broad smile. 'That's no good, is it, George?'

'No good at all,' the other man responds.

'I can see we'll have to do something about that.'

Webster then takes his wallet from his pocket and Michael pulls the moneybag open. He watches as Webster drops some large coins into the bag. When the last of the coins has fallen, Michael pulls on the string that closes the bag and says thank you. Then, just as he is about to turn and leave, Webster pulls a note from his wallet, folds it over and pushes it into the breast pocket of Michael's shirt.

'And there,' he adds. 'There's a little extra. For being such a good team man and coming all this way to find us.'

Michael simply stares back at Webster. He couldn't see the note properly, but he saw the colour. And he knows from the colour that Webster has just placed a ten-pound note in his pocket. A look of silent, but unequivocal understanding passes between the three of them. The coins are there for the club, the note is for Michael's silence.

Their business concluded, Webster inquires if he knows his way back to the front gate. Michael nods and turns to leave, his eyes falling on the green canvas tarpaulin before doing so.

At the front gate he swings about and looks back at the house and the grounds, everything as still and quiet as it was when he arrived a mere ten or fifteen minutes before. But he has travelled far in that ten or fifteen minutes. He has travelled to another country — this other country that exists behind the walls of Webster's mansion and he wouldn't be surprised to now learn that it was days, not minutes, that he was away.

40.

The Empty Home

In the late afternoon the Home ought to have been at its busiest. The windows should be lit with a summery glow, there ought to be voices, silhouettes passing behind curtained squares of yellow light. But there is none of that. The Home is still and silent. A shell, the life it once contained gone.

A week before he could never have stepped onto the circular gravel driveway of the Home and strolled about its gardens, but now he does. The cottages are quiet, the trees motionless on a still summer's day. Michael is the only moving figure in that afternoon glow, and he moves slowly and respectfully. The ground-floor doors, the verandah, the cast-iron balcony are all in partial shadow. The late sun catches the white railing of the balcony, the windows are dark and soon the whole house will be sleeping by itself, back from the street, in the vast expanse of its own night. If houses dream, surely this one does.

Once it was where Kathleen Marsden lived, now it houses the memories of when she did. He has her letter in his drawer at home. The first love letter she has ever written, the first he has ever received. It is a love letter, but a practical one acknowledging that the place to which she has been thrown may just as well be on the other side of the earth as the other side of the city; a letter of farewell as much as love. And as he stands in the grounds, he remembers her smile that bright Saturday morning when he came to see her play.

If he wanted he could climb the cast-iron column onto the balcony, stare into the window that was once hers and onto the white metal bed that will still be there and which was silent witness to the private life of Kathleen Marsden.

The Home has been empty for over a week and has the look of a house that has only just been vacated. Small objects here and there — a comb, a book, a woollen hat, either under a shrub or left lying on a step — all bear the signs of a recent departure. He can imagine the orderly confusion. Girls, matrons and removalists. Bags filled with everything they have. The small girls all talking at once, the older girls, who have had no other home but this, taking one last look. He can imagine all this with only the crunch of the gravel under his sandshoes to disturb his thoughts and the insistent, distant sound of a hammer on some far-off tin roof.

He wants to see if the place has changed, and it has. He also wants to know if the mystery has gone, and it hasn't. There is more of it. This will always be the place where he found something other than speed to fill his days and fill his mind, where Kathleen Marsden became Kate, and he discovered that there were other gifts in life to be given and received. And when the time comes, when he is able to put things together a little more clearly than he can now, he will understand that this is also the place where he fell just that little bit in love with Kathleen Marsden, and just that little bit out of love with the world of speed. In time, but not yet. For the realisation is still travelling towards him, slowly, like the old red rattlers that creep out of the city on days such as this and lumber up those deceptive inclines that lead into his suburb. At the moment he still takes it for granted that he is at his happiest when walking back along his run to his bowling mark.

He will not see Kathleen Marsden again. And it is not simply the distance between them. All that was ever going to happen has happened. She discovered for the first time in her life the ordinary happiness of knowing that there really was someone out there after all. Someone outside the confines of the Home who would come to watch her play and to whom she could go and for whom she could release the smile that she knew was somewhere inside her just waiting for its time and place of release; someone with whom she could feel less thrown. And he too had glimpsed for the first time that there was something out there beyond the sealed, self-enclosed world of speed. That the walls and towers of that world he had constructed and over which he had complete control could crumble one hot afternoon in a disused stable, and that a part of him would watch it all fall down and not care. There was another world entirely out there, and if he really wanted to, he could let it in.

This was their gift to each other. Now, the gift was given, and there was nothing left to be done. It was enough to know that if such moments could happen once, they could happen again. The moment at the hayride when she had read his thoughts, the afternoon in the heat of the old stable when he silently acknowledged that *here* was fine, *here* was good and all the yearning to be elsewhere could finally stop. When he suddenly wasn't exclusively living for that faraway moment when he would feel the ripple of the perfect delivery pass through him and which would tell him that he had the gift of speed. When he wasn't straining towards that moment with all his strength, but happy to simply stand still and not want anything more or wish to be anywhere else. It is another way of doing things that makes him feel light in his feet and legs and shoulders. A lightness of being that makes him aware for the first time of the weight he carries round with him, that he never knew was there. But at this moment it is still just a glimpse. And he might be told (on this particular evening in front of the empty Home with Webster's ten-pound note still stuffed in his pocket) that his world has shifted, that he has been nudged in ways that he hadn't counted on when the summer began, but he won't hear because he's not yet ready to hear — and that lumbering red rattler that is carrying the news is still travelling towards him up those deceptive inclines that lead into the suburb.

41.

A Thief in Your Own Home

It's come to this. Games. Tricks. Michael wanders
freely around the grounds of what once was St
Catherine's Girls' Home, Vic works in the front
garden in khaki shorts and sandals, and Rita slowly
opens the drawer in which Vic keeps his
handkerchiefs, cork-tipped cigarettes and spare
change. Vic is clearly visible through the bedroom
windows. She can see him, he can't see her. She's
opened this drawer a hundred times before and never
felt like a thief, but today she does. It is the guilt doing
all this, she tells herself — the slow tentative manner
in which she opens the drawer, the way she looks
about the room to make sure she is still alone in the
house (or that his mother hasn't wandered out of her
room again), and the cautious way she picks through

the spare change and the cigarettes until she finds what she wants. It is at the very bottom, underneath one of the notepads in which he writes those odd bits of poems and quotes from books. She wasn't looking the first time, but now she is. And, for this reason, she feels like a thief in her own home.

She takes the postcard out from under the notepad. The real estate agent's card is under the postcard. It might mean something, it might mean nothing. She stares at the postcard and once again realises how much she likes the look of this town. Slowly, slyly, she slips them both into her dress pocket and smooths the contents of the drawer, to make it look like no one has been there — then wonders if, because everything looks so orderly and neat, that it looks like someone has. But she shuts the drawer firmly. If it means something she will hear, if it doesn't she won't.

It is a sad communication, but a communication all the same. She walks through the kitchen to the bin. It's come to this, games and tricks. But sometimes you've got to know these things, haven't you? Surely everybody comes across these odd little bits and pieces, those little things that tell a wife something about her husband's life that her husband never told her, or those things that tell a husband something about his wife's life that she never let on about. Little things, but things that nag at you until you end up feeling like a thief in your own home. This happens to everyone, even the happy couples. It's like taking two photographs. Everybody does it. It doesn't mean anything. Time passes. And before you know it you're having a quiet laugh to yourself and it's soon forgotten.

Later that afternoon, the gardening done, Vic goes to his drawer for the cork-tipped cigarettes, and from the moment he opens it he knows that something is different. More than different, wrong. The contents of the drawer either look too neat or too deliberately ruffled. Whatever, a hand other than his has been here today. At first he thinks of Michael taking his cigarettes. But Michael, to the best of his knowledge, doesn't smoke. Then he counts the loose change, and it all seems to be there. But something is gone. It is only when he picks up the notepad at the bottom of the drawer that he realises what it is, and knows straight away who took it.

He is motionless, his eyes fixed on the drawer, but blank. While they were there, in the drawer in this open way, these cards were not an issue. And they weren't at first. He just threw them there when he'd come back from his trip, with some vague notion of returning one day to this place, to visit or stay. He didn't know. It was only in the weeks that followed that the memory of the town and the idea of living there got into his bones and took hold — so much so that he knew that one day he would indeed return. By then it was too late to take the cards away and hide them somewhere, because that would look suspicious. So he left them there in his drawer, in this open manner. A couple of harmless mementos.

Now this. It is, he acknowledges, a communication. Rita's way of asking a question because she needs badly to know the answer. But it is not a question she can just come out and ask herself, is it? Not her. Not them. So, she has found this way of posing the question to Vic. He knows straight away that his answer can take one of two forms. He can say something, or he can say nothing.

If he says something he may, by his willingness to speak of them in an open way, confirm that the cards are simply harmless mementos. In such an event his tone would be casual and light. She would look up from her magazine and either know something about their disappearance or not. And the matter would be closed. But he also knows that it would be a dangerous conversation to begin, because it may continue and he could never be sure just where it might end up. There may be more questions, and he may have some awkward explaining to do. Of course, there is only one response. And that is to say nothing.

The question has been asked, and he will answer with silence; the way they do in this house.

He removes the cork-tipped cigarettes from the drawer, then leaves the bedroom. Rita is sitting in the lounge room reading a magazine. When he suggests that they open the windows to let the breeze through she looks up over her magazine and fixes his eyes for a moment in silent scrutiny. She reads his look, concludes that he has either noticed or he hasn't (Vic is not sure), then she nods.

There. It is done. They have communicated. It is, he reflects, a sad communication, but it is done, and as he lights the cigarette, he notes it has been done in the manner of the house. No one and nothing has been disturbed, except for the venetian blinds responding to the late-afternoon breeze.

42.

Lindsay Hassett's Sports Store

That evening Michael sits in his room examining the ten-pound note. He has seen ten-pound notes before but never owned one. The note had been slipped into his shirt pocket almost as an afterthought, but he knows it isn't. The question Michael goes over and over again in his room is what to do with the money. He could give it to the club, to the team. He was, after all, collecting for the club, and had it not been for the club he would not have been on Webster's property in the first place. So the club should get it. Really. But there were two payments, he points out to himself while dragging the edge of the note across his cheek as if he were shaving (which he now does irregularly). One for the club, one for Michael. And even when Webster had called him a good team man, it was said in such a way that suggested Webster had found, in Michael, one of his own, someone who goes alone and prefers it that way. A tone that suggested a man would be a fool to play for the team, that if he had any brains at all he would take the money and keep quiet, and that he best looked after the team by looking after himself. Webster, had never played for the team — which is why he is Webster and everybody else is just everybody else. He could call it Webster's gift, but it is not a gift. Webster does not give gifts. Although he doesn't know the Websters of the world, all the other Websters, that is, he knows that they're out there and that they don't give gifts.

He will give the coins to the club and keep the paper for himself. It has fallen into his lap with the neatness of something that was destined. It is out of his hands. The money has a pre-determined purpose and he will see that it meets its destiny.

Outside, through the open louvre windows of his room, the voice of Mrs Barlow carries across the fence, across the yard, and across the whole suburb for all he knows. The house is wrong, she wails. The street is ghastly. The suburb is stuck out on the edge of the world. She is ashamed of the address. Ashamed of him. It is always the same. He knows it all by heart now. Further up the street Bruckner's dog howls periodically in the still night to the accompaniment of Younger's hammer. He is out late, Albert Younger, with nothing better to do than piece the scraps of his house together.

Michael snaps to his feet, slips the ten-pound note into the old brown wallet he inherited from his father, and places the wallet on his bedside table. The club clinic, the training session for which he has practised throughout the summer, is now only days away. The ten-pound note has fallen into his pocket with the neatness of things destined to be. So when he steps out onto that wide, green oval in two days he will have feet. And with the feet will come speed, and everything else.

The next day the basement shop is cool and quiet like a library. Summers will come and go, but the smell of this shop in the years ahead will always be synonymous with the smell of summers past and of afternoons that stretch out forever and drive people underground. Michael has come straight from school. He knows what he wants. As he moves through the shop the radio voice of Hassett blends with the sleepy tranquillity of the place. He passes the sleeveless sweaters that can only be found here, passes the trousers and caps and socks, and stops at the boots.

They are white, new and crisp, and the rich smell of fresh leather rises from the boxes before him much as it does from a new football. He knows exactly which boots he wants, drops his school bag on the floor and soon finds them. But something is wrong. Some part of him suspected throughout the day that there was always going to be something wrong because it was so late in the season. As much as he tries he can't find his size, the boots that were here the last time he was in the shop are gone. There is no size even near his. They are either children's boots or giant's boots. He lightly stamps his foot on the floor, enough to disturb things.

He hears Hassett's voice and wonders who the question might be addressed to when he realises that Hassett is standing beside him.

'Can I help you?' he is saying, and Michael turns slowly towards him attempting to simultaneously register the nearness of Hassett as well as the content of his question. Hassett is patient, a quiet smile in his eyes, and Michael is surprised and pleased to see that the twinkle the newspaper articles refer to is there in life. It is while he is contemplating this that he suddenly blurts out a two-word response to the question.

'The boots.'

'Yes?'

'They're too big, or too small.'

Hassett nods as he eyes Michael's feet, then checks the sizes printed on the remaining boxes.

'That's right. You're a common size.'

'Do you have any more?' Michael persists.

'No.'

'But you'll get more in?'

Hassett shakes his head.

'You're out of luck, I'm afraid.'

How can Michael tell him that all summer he has contemplated those boots. That if he is to have feet, he must have them. For a moment his annoyance — the same helpless childish rage that consumed so many of his father's boozy Saturday nights — controls him. For a moment he forgets that he is talking to the man who was once captain of Australia. For a moment the patience and genial understanding of Hassett threaten to drive Michael up the walls of his crummy little basement shop — as does the famous twinkle in Hassett's eyes, and suddenly Michael is behaving as if Hassett were just another shop assistant who doesn't know his job.

'Why not?' Michael stammers, rousing the curiosity of the shop.

Hassett remains calm, his manner still genial, the twinkle still in his eyes, as he shakes his head a little sadly.

'It's the end of the season.'

Michael stands, his hands on his hips, staring at the floor, without speaking.

'You're a bowler?'

'Yes.' Michael doesn't even look up.

It is in the short silence that follows, while Michael is looking down at the floor, that he sees them. Boots. Not the boots that he wants, but his size and he wonders why he didn't notice them before. He impulsively reaches out and holds one up.

'These?'

'They're batsman's boots,' Hassett says, all patience and geniality.

'Does it matter?' Michael asks, but Hassett shakes his head.

'They're too heavy. Look, there's no spikes in the heels. They're batsman's boots.'

Hassett takes the boot from Michael as if removing an unnecessary temptation and places it back in its box. He looks up from the boots with a smile on his face.

'You'd be a fool to buy them. And I'd be a crook to sell them to you.'

It is then that another customer catches his eye and he is gone. The matter of the boots is concluded.

But Michael doesn't move. He must have them. When nobody is watching him he tries them on. They fit. Even with his grey school socks they fit. He places them back in the box and waits until Hassett is occupied at the other end of the shop discussing bats. He is talking to a man of his own vintage, and from the tone of their conversation he can tell that they will go on for some time. It's enough for Michael to slip quietly up to the counter, where an assistant is standing at the cash register. Enough to pass the ten-pound note across and slip out up the stairs.

In the late-afternoon glare, Michael places the boots in his school bag, and as he walks up the street to the gaping mouth of the station, he carries more than boots in his bag. He carries his feet in his bag. The feet that will give him speed. The speed that will turn heads.

43.

The Distinguished Guest

While Michael is buying his boots, and while Webster takes yet another afternoon off to clean the engine of his car, Rita is waiting for Black to arrive. When a doctor enters a house the kitchen should be clean, the magazines stacked neatly on the lounge-room table, and a fresh towel placed in the bathroom. When the doctor's dust-covered jeep pulls up at the front of the house, Rita checks everything one more time, because it's not often the doctor calls. As he strolls up the gravel path, gazing at the birds passing overhead and the bright summer sky above, she puzzles over the easy, loping stride of this large man, whose face has grown puffy in the years they've all been here. He looks as though he could do with a good visit to the doctor himself.

There is no urgency to his walk, and it was the same when Vic had his first fit all those years ago. He stops and marvels at the flight of wild ducks on their way to the rubbish tip just north of the suburb. This is his way of going from a cold, to a death, and back to a cold again without getting too involved. She watches him walk to the front door, but doesn't move even though she can see him perfectly well through the lounge-room window. No, she watches and she waits until he knocks, because to anticipate his knocking is to signal that his arrival is much waited upon — and the fresh towels in the bathroom would acquire the look of special-occasion towels (not an everyday occurrence) — and he will know that he is the occasion. Rita is not prepared to let him know this — and there is no emergency — so she waits until he knocks a second time then leaves her place by the lounge-room window, where she has had a perfect view of everything.

'She's here,' Rita says after greeting Black and pointing to the closed door just behind them.

Inside that dark room, shut up against the afternoon sun, the tall, stooping doctor with the black carrying case of his trade smiles at the small, bony woman sitting up in the bed, and asks soft, reassuring questions about her hip and back. The old woman, who likes a chat, is explaining to him for the third or fourth time what a silly thing it was for her to fall over like that. As he goes about his business of prodding and tapping and listening, Black reassures her that it can happen to anybody and that she shouldn't blame her age. Everybody falls over — and everybody gets up again.

And then, as if it were an afterthought, as if the main examination of the morning were complete and only the small, trivial matters needed to be attended to, he casually turns to her in the semi-darkness.

'Now, let's have a look at that throat.'

Like a white-haired girl eager to be of assistance, she opens her mouth wide as he shines a small, doctor's torch down her throat. There is a low humming sound coming from deep down in his throat, casual, almost distracted, as if only one part of his mind is concentrating on the matter at hand, while another part is concentrating on something else altogether. She shuts her mouth, he switches the small torch off, stares briefly at the ceiling, then switches the torch on again and asks the old woman to open her mouth once more. And Mary obliges once again. Black motions to Rita with his forefinger and calls her to his side. At first she wonders why but then she sees the swollen creepers flourishing in pink triumph and is instantly sick in the heart.

When the examination is finished Mary shuts her mouth, then reaches for a butterscotch from the table beside her. Crunching on the sweet, her teeth still strong, she asks about her hip and he tells her it will mend, but slowly. She must be patient, and she nods as if to say that she expected him to say exactly that, that he would tell her what they all tell her, that in age, all things mend slowly — or not at all.

On the front porch, with the bedroom door well shut behind them, Black turns to Rita with a quiet certainty in his eyes.

'I don't think Grandma will be with us much longer.'

Rita asks how much longer, and he says not long, perhaps even days, for decline can be swift and dramatic.

'She thinks it's a summer cold,' says Rita, aware of the fact that she too is now taking in the sky and the birds.

Black nods and tells Rita that there is no reason to change her mind. Let her keep thinking that, it will change nothing. Rita tells him that she craves cold beer in the afternoons and evenings and Black tells her that Grandma can have all the cold beer she wants.

Behind the wheel, Black is oblivious of the street and the suburb. It always comes to this. In the end. The Distinguished Guest is suddenly there, walking alongside us, decked out in his best clothes. An affable assistant. Possibly with an urbane quip or two tucked up the sleeve of his best suit. But Mr James, Black reflects, was never a doctor, and he never saw the other side of this Distinguished Guest — the ruffian with more than a few too many stingers inside him who won't take no for an answer, and whose invitation is more than likely followed by a belch than a gentle quip. This is the side that Black sees.

And as much as his job brings him face to face with the ruffian inside the Distinguished Guest, he is never at ease in his company or able to accommodate him. It is always like this. Inside the neat, white house he has just left is an old woman whose life has been lived and who will soon be gone. Gone. It could be somewhere, it could be nowhere. It is all in the way you say it. And this, it always occurs to Black, is where it all breaks down; all those fine books and fine words he so admires. The Distinguished Guest goes where words can't and never will go, and the cold look of disdain on his face tells you all you need to know about what he thinks of words.

44.

Mrs Webster at the Bedroom Windows

Something draws Mrs Webster to the bedroom windows, a sound so low that it gives every impression of not wanting to bring attention to itself. And because of this, Mrs Webster has noticed it. She looks down into the gardens and sees something move. At first she takes it to be a long shadow, cast by the moonlight across the circular driveway. Then she realises that this shadow is not swaying the way shadows do, but leaving the house altogether.

She pulls the curtains back and watches the progress of a car. It is her husband's one indulgence. A game they play. He casually announces to her that he is working late and will sleep in the guest room. She always nods as though it makes perfect sense. But behind the nod there is a smile that he never sees. She parts the lace curtains. The windows of the car are dark, the driver hidden behind the glass. His indulgence had only ever broken her sleep once, a few years ago, and never again. Until tonight.

A harmless thing, she tells herself, as the long, low shadow of his car sweeps out along the driveway through the blue gardens. Because the car didn't want to be heard, she heard it. For a moment she wonders if it means anything. She is a practical person, untouched by superstition. All the same, it is not like her to be standing by the windows this late and she lingers at the curtains when the car is gone a little longer than need be.

The long, low nose of the car parts the night. The houses are in darkness, the shops are shut, and the beast is loose. Its headlights carefully eye each intersection and corner. It is only as he passes the two towers of the flour mills (brilliant in the moonlight) and turns left into one of the two main streets of the suburb — the one street that will give him an unimpeded, straight stretch of road — that the eight perfectly cleaned and tuned cylinders of the car growl and rumble into primitive life.

Webster is perfectly still as he plunges the accelerator to the floor. He sinks into the seat, his head resting back, his eyes on the road, and merges with the car. He eases back slightly at the one curve in the road, the dogleg at the corner where St Matthew's sits, its bells silent, then flattens the accelerator once again for the mile-long stretch of road that runs down to where the suburb officially ends. It will take less than a minute and during that time car and driver will be one. For those fifty precious seconds the driver totally forgets who he is, what he is and where he is. He merges with the car, with the seat, the pedals and the internal workings of the engine itself. He becomes the car. He becomes speed and is transformed into sheer phenomenon.

The deep sleep of the suburb is undisturbed throughout. Just as nothing is stirred when the car turns and completes its return journey, before preparing to slip once again into the anonymous dark streets at the far end of the suburb that were once thistle and grass.

But instead of returning home, Webster does something he has never done before. He brings the car round on the dark, silent street that runs alongside the flour mills. Webster is not satisfied, the annihilation he craved, not complete. Once more he points the low, dark hood of the car out towards the darkness at the edge of the suburb where his ride will take him. Out to where the Scotch thistles and khaki grass still cover the land and there is space enough to accelerate into life or into death one more time.

45.

Speed

The lights of a house don't need to be on for a house to be stirred. And just because the lights of a house are off, it doesn't mean that the occupants are sleeping. The lights don't mean anything. Vic has been awake for hours. He is normally a deep sleeper, someone who can fall asleep anywhere. It is, he suspects, something he learnt on those long nights when his engine had broken down or the tracks were blocked up ahead and there was nothing else for it but to get what sleep there was to be had. And if you can learn to sleep bolt upright in a driver's seat with only the cabin windows to rest your head on, you can sleep anywhere. But not tonight.

He hears it, out to the north of the suburb, that familiar distant growl. At first, its visits were irregular, often months apart. This was how it was for years. Just when he thought it had gone away and died a natural death, it was back. Now, he hears it more and more. And whereas once there was something magnificent in its growl, something simple and elemental, there isn't now. It was still the same car and presumably the same driver you would raise your hat to if hats were back in fashion — but something had gone from the whole caper. And he couldn't put his finger on it.

Then it occurred to him that it wasn't the sound of the car that was different — it was him. It was because in his heart of hearts he knew he was leaving everything — the house, suburb, the whole shooting match. Physically still here, but where it matters, all but gone. The sound of the car fades, drifts like it always does, back into that corner of the suburb from which it comes, its anonymity all part of its mystery. But then, when the sound is gone, the driver does something he has never done before. He turns the car around and the whole thing starts all over again. It is uncharacteristic, and Vic is alert and awake, listening as intently as he always did in the days when the sound first drove into his nights.

The low groan, the roar of the acceleration, the rattle of the bedroom venetians as it passes out there on the main road, the long, slow fading of the engine until it becomes a low hum are all there again. But this time it tapers into silence. This time he doesn't hear the car coming round for the return journey. This time there is only silence. And as much as he listens and waits, the silence remains.

Vic wants to stay awake so that he can confirm its return (for he is absurdly concerned), but the sleep that he has been denied all night catches up with him.

He wakes in daylight, oddly troubled.

When Vic eventually learns of the car's fate he will take the story personally, for what it will tell him is that the time for shooting through is near. That one can stay on in a place like this for only so long. That the suburb has changed and can no longer absorb the things it could when it was on the frontier. A suburb is tamed by time, subdued by its own speed. In the flicker of a bored eye, a paddock becomes a suburb, the frontier shifts, and all the types that the place was once wild enough to take in, must either adapt or go.

In the days that follow — through talk and a large notice in the local newspaper (the same newspaper that will also carry a photograph of the ex-detective, Gannon, standing in front of a city court) — word will filter through the suburb that Webster, the factory, is dead. A giant, the local paper will write, has gone. And the suburb will agree. Webster the factory has gone. Undone by speed. Even those who suffered under him — those who were abused by him on the factory floor, those who broke under his intolerance, who couldn't keep pace with him, or those who simply didn't like him — will mourn him, even weep for him. Webster, the factory, they will note, is gone. And something, a centre they never knew was there until it wasn't, will be gone from their lives. Everybody chooses differently when the time comes. Webster's is a death Vic will instantly respect upon hearing of it. The death of one of those who come and go on their own terms. And if hats were back in fashion, he would indeed still raise his to a fellow sentimentalist.

46.

A Bowler in Batsman's Boots

On the day the suburb wakes to the death of Webster, Michael is contemplating the district club oval — a field so completely green and thick with grass that it could easily have sprung from a book and he, Michael, were about to step onto one of its pages. He pauses at the gate — his new boots in his school bag — and dwells on the curve of the white picket fence surrounding the oval before taking that first step into the world of the great Lindwall. For it is on playing fields such as these that he will find them all, those distant figures that fed his youth. And it is at this moment, before stepping over the gutter and onto the oval, that he appreciates, for the first time, the deeply thrilling private joy his father must have known when his dream was so close that he could almost see his name on the roster board of the Big Wheel drivers.

As he crosses the ground he is sure that all the speed that is within him could be released on grounds such as these.

At the nets he sees for the first time pitches that are neither concrete nor gravel nor sand nor dirt, but turf. He bends down on one knee to open his school bag and take his boots out. As he puts the new white boots on the grass, something turns his head and he feels the impulse to look about. When he does, he sees it, close up, for the first time. Speed. One moment he is holding his boots in mid-air, the next he has placed them on the ground. But in that time an anonymous white arm has whipped over and a dull red ball has covered the length of the pitch, soundlessly bouncing off the back of the nets. It is only a glimpse, and he has never seen speed close at hand before, but it is unmistakable. Whoever owns that anonymous white arm has the gift of speed. All around him heads are turning and watching closely as the boy runs in once more. Michael too. And as he watches the whole process this time — the run, the approach and the delivery — he realises it is not just the boy's speed that is turning heads, it is the way he does it. An action too perfect to have been learnt. This boy has never studied anybody, Michael is sure of that. Why he is sure, he doesn't know. But he is. Michael watches again and again, and every time it is the same — smooth, easy and perfect — too perfect to have been studied. The more he watches, the more he realises he is watching a natural. He has heard of naturals, those for whom everything falls into place because it is written into them. This action, this ease, this speed, are written into the arms and legs and back and brain of the natural. It is his gift and he is as unaware of it as a bird is of flying — or Kathleen Marsden of the brightness she brings with her. He is watching one of those for whom everything effortlessly falls into place — girlfriends, conversation, the prompt obedience with which a cigarette ejects itself from a soft pack with one flick of the finger. Life, he suspects, is full of naturals. And this bowler, whose speed is turning heads, does not have to look into books or photographs or films to see a picture of what he wants to become. He simply is. He simply does. And if you were to ask him how he does it, he would not be able to tell you. But Michael could. He knows he could, and he wishes so dearly that he couldn't.

The boots glow on the glowing grass. The *clock clock* of bats and balls, the grunts, the comments of coaches and senior players carry across the nets and in from the curved lines of fieldsmen out on the ground. The first thing he notes is that the boots are heavier than his worn-out sandshoes, heavier than his school shoes. Heavier than anything he has worn. But heavy or not, these boots will give him feet, and as he picks up a ball from a metal bucket — a leather ball — a senior player directs him to a far net.

The natural is still turning heads and as Michael marks out the fifteen paces of his run he is determined to do the same. For if you don't turn heads, you don't have speed, and if you don't have speed you have nothing and all the effort was for nothing. It has taken years to arrive at this point and as he stands at the top of his run he feels those years, and they are heavier than his boots. It has come down to this. To the next hour. If he is to turn heads, he must do it now.

As he stands ball in hand waiting to begin, all the wisdom of those years deserts him. The voice of the great Lindwall, the voice that tells him to begin slowly, to build speed gradually and not to over-stretch at delivery, is nowhere to be heard as he starts his run to the crease. He hears none of their voices, all of those flickering figures in black and white who taught him. He is conscious only of the extra weight of his boots, of how slow and leaden his steps are, and of the need to push his legs, to lift his feet, to run fast. When he reaches his delivery stride he feels, for an alarming moment, as though his raised left leg, with the extra weight of the boot attached, just might continue on through the air and down the pitch without him. He is not even aware of where the ball has landed. Again and again, ball after ball, he is aware only of the need to push his legs. Faster than the time before, then faster again. But it is all wrong. More wrong than it has ever been, yet he seems powerless to stop it. Each time he releases the ball there is no sound of speed. Heads do not turn. And he determines, as he stamps back to the top of his run, that this time, with this ball, he will turn heads and everything will be as it should. The dream will meet reality, and somewhere in the northern distance of his suburb, life will come to a stop and everyone will be forced to agree that the boy has the gift of speed.

It is almost as though he hears the sound before he feels the pain. He hears it go off like the crack of a rifle at close range. And then the pain, as if, indeed, he has been shot in the back. And this pain is so immense, he knows immediately that the damage is as immense as the pain. This is not the dull pain of the past that everybody expects and that soon goes away. This is pain the likes of which he has never felt before, and he knows without question that something is wrong in a way that it has never been wrong before.

The ball tumbles from his hand and lands just a few feet in front of him, and he grasps his back as if preventing himself from snapping in two. It is not possible for him to stand alone without crumbling to the ground and soon he is being supported by arms, either side of him, and is being led from the training nets. It has all been both fast and slow — the long explosion of pain, the spectacularly slow tumble of the ball from his fingers, the creeping exit from the nets — and yet all over in a devastating flash. It is only then, as he is being led from the nets, the crack of the rifle shot still ringing in his ears, his face creased with the pain, that he notices for the first time that heads are turning.

Away from the nets he attempts to lie back on the soft, glowing grass. Someone is asking him where the pain is. He touches his lower back, then adds that it is everywhere. And as he is talking to these two senior players one of them suddenly points to his boots and says, what are they? And Michael replies that they're his boots and the senior player says he can see that — but adds that they are batsman's boots. Doesn't he know that? They are not made for bowling and he should not be bowling in them. Michael nods and as he is nodding the player asks him what crook sold the boots to him and Michael says nothing.

Someone brings his bag. Someone else takes his boots off, and Michael feels the weight drop from his feet, instantly wishing he'd bowled in his sandshoes and cursing Webster's ten-pound note. Soon the boots are in his bag and, in time, he is able to limp from the ground, slowly and uncertainly, every turn of the head, every step that he takes executed with the deliberation of an old man. He steps slowly over the gutter at the boundary, off the field and back onto the concrete race he had walked up less than half an hour before, when everything was still in front of him and the ground glowed in the late-afternoon sun, the way ovals glow in books.

That evening Michael is standing in his yard staring at the back fence. The white paint representing the three stumps is old now and the paint is an over-milked tea colour in the dull, orange light. The pain in his back is not so bad if he doesn't move, but he forgets this and leans quickly, impulsively to his right to peak through a hole in the fence where the paling has cracked. Through the gap he can see the children in the house behind his playing in a portable, plastic pool, splashing and spraying water into the air, chasing each other around the lawn, their bodies twisting into all sorts of impossible positions then snapping back to normal with elastic ease. As he watches them tumbling in and out of the plastic pool, he feels old at sixteen. Nobody should feel old at sixteen. But the elasticity has gone from his body and he feels at that moment as if all his summers are over.

The sounds of the suburb crowd round him. Mrs Barlow is quiet, their house is quiet, apart from the occasional low coughing of Mr Barlow and their television floating through the opened windows and across the yard to where Michael is standing. Somewhere a flyscreen door slams just that little harder than it ought to. There is a sudden gust of canned laughter, a chorus of squeals in the night, the distant rattle of the city-bound train that always sounds empty. His summer is over, and he hears them all now, these distractions that he ought not to hear because there is nothing to concentrate on. And he suddenly feels not only absurdly old, but lonely. And not the kind of loneliness that makes him wish that Kathleen Marsden were still there. It is not that kind of loneliness — if he were to summon her up and have her stand with him now, he would not be any less lonely. This new kind of loneliness would still be with him, and his summer would still be over, no matter who was standing with him.

47.

The Lesson of Fred Trueman

Early the next morning, his slipped discs back in place, Michael is sitting in Black's rooms and the doctor is pointing to an X-ray of his back. Black is saying that Michael's back shows the signs of wear that one might expect to see in a back fifteen years older — or more. And a labourer at that. Not a sixteen-year-old student. He turns from the X-ray and asks — with a clear sense of incredulity — what on earth the young Michael has been up to. And Michael says, quite calmly, that he has been playing cricket.

Black stares at Michael for a long time, calculating the sheer frequency and intensity of playing required to do this kind of damage, then nods slowly to himself. He knows the family. He knows the house, Vic, Rita and their dying grandmother in the spare room who thinks she's got a summer cold. He knows them all and continues nodding before speaking in a quiet, unemotional voice. Did Michael not feel pain before the discs were thrown out? his doctor asks. And Michael nods, with the same, quiet calm, that he did feel pain. Yes. A certain amount, but adds that everybody expects a certain amount of pain, that you can't have speed without pain; but even as he says it he knows that this is the talk of the old Michael — the Michael who desired speed enough to almost break his back.

Black shifts and swivels in his seat and offers one, simple piece of advice.

'Stop.'

But it is said in such a way that Michael is left in no doubt that it is not a piece of advice, but an order.

'Stop playing.'

A week before, even a few days before, obeying such an order would have been unthinkable. Black might just as well have asked him to stop breathing. But today Michael takes it calmly, and stares at the floor, nodding.

'Give it up now,' Black continues, 'this ... madness. Unless you want to be a cripple at thirty, or forty.' He shrugs. 'Whenever it all finally catches up with you and you find yourself shuffling about like an old man when you're not. Oh, by all means,' he goes on, 'play for fun. For amusement. But whatever you've been up to, give it away now.'

Michael could say that he has never played for amusement, or just for the fun of it. And there is a part of him that now acknowledges that he really ought to have been. It is then, in Black's surgery, with the X-ray of his prematurely aged and worn back pinned to the screen, that the face of Fred Trueman comes to mind. For it was always the face of Freddie Trueman that caught his eye, not the bowler's style. It was a face that was always grinning, or always seemed on the point of a grin. A face that was always entertaining the possibility of a harmless little prank that might amuse everybody — or a childish and stupid one that wouldn't amuse anybody but Freddie Trueman himself. He imagines the face of Fred Trueman out there on the ground, a joker with a fight in his eyes, a grin all right, with the street fighter not far behind. Michael had no doubt there would be days when you would hate Fred Trueman and his stupid larking about, but the hatred wouldn't last. Trueman's face reminded you that amid all the training, the effort, the long days in the field that never seemed to end and the sheer slog of it all, there was fun to be had. And if you weren't having fun, then what were you doing?

Looking at the game through the eyes of Fred Trueman, everything seemed like a giant lark. Oh, you never took it easy and you never stopped giving everything you had — he has the face of someone who loves every second that he is in the game — but it's also the face of someone who would be quick to tell you not to leave your grin at the gate when you go out to play.

This is the lesson of Fred Trueman. But is it Fred or Freddie? For Trueman has two names, it seems to Michael. Fred for when he's got the ball in his hand and he's running straight at you with that crazy look in his eyes, as if he'd dearly love to dispense with the ball altogether and just keep running, past the popping crease, down the pitch, right up to you and knock your block off. Dispense with the ball, the bat, and all the jolly nice talk that comes with the game that merely gets in the way of what you really want to do — knock the batsman's block off. Just once. That's Fred. Freddie, Michael imagines, is the bloke with his hands on his hips with plenty to say after he's made you look pretty silly. He hasn't knocked your block off. All the same, he's got plenty to say, and in such a way that suggests one day he just might.

Michael has never met Fred Trueman and he never will, but this is what the face of Fred Trueman tells him when he looks at it in books and magazines. As he is walking to the railway station from Black's surgery, he wonders why the lesson of Fred Trueman never sank in until this day. And, with that, he wonders if it had sunk in a little earlier, whether it would have made any difference. Whether he would have been up to the lesson of Fred Trueman — who had the gift of fun — and whether he would have relaxed every now and then and made things just a little bit easier on himself. Whether it would have mattered, and whether his long run to the crease would have been changed, minutely, but minutely enough to give him the gift he'd so desired but never won, because he forgot to laugh along the way.

48.

A Salute

There are many summer smells to Michael — the reek of sweet chewing gum in a crowded car; the stench that follows when a pub door suddenly swings open; the perfumes and the aftershave that drenched the air before all the parties of his youth, the parties that started well and always ended up wrong. These are the smells of summer that will always remain sad ones. That he is aware of too often. But this morning the smell of summer is good, in spite of the X-rays depicting his damaged back he'd seen an hour before in the doctor's surgery. Perhaps it is because of this, because he is released from it all now, that this morning the smell of summer is good as it floats through the low hanging trees and across the lawns towards Michael. It is early morning and the real heat hasn't arrived yet. The park sparkles and a light breeze, carrying with it the rich scent of damp lawn where the sprinklers have been, floats through the trees towards him.

The high brick walls of the Melbourne Cricket Ground rise up before him. Puffs of cloud come and go and the coloured flags on top of the stands flutter under a slowly moving sky. It is Wednesday and Michael has skipped school. The crowds haven't yet arrived but Michael is not here this early to beat the crowds, which he knows will come for this last day of the series. Nor has he come this early so that he may secure a good seat. Behind the red brick of the Members Stand, enclosed by a picket fence, is the open quadrangle where the practice nets are. The players from both sides come here before each day's play and Michael has come to watch.

Small groups of spectators — fathers and their children, boys in the school uniforms, who, like Michael, have taken the day off, and loners — gather near the nets even though the players have not yet arrived. The day will be a stinker, the crowds will come and the ground will barely contain its many guests. The city will, for the day, have the look of an evacuated town. He carries his school bag over his shoulder and is aimlessly wandering past the nets, staring up at the Members Stand, when a door opens. He hears a ripple of comment, and from the corner of his eye he catches a glimpse of flannels and colour. When he lowers his gaze he is staring directly at the faces he knows so well from television, books and newspapers. But they have never looked so far away as they do, right now, in front of him.

A close group, they talk softly as they make their way to the practice nets. Michael stands perfectly still and watches them pass by in front of him. Their heads are lowered. There are no smiles. They are serious. They could almost be a group of businessmen going to work, not cricketers, not the lucky ones who have been lifted up and swept away from their streets and suburbs into the great, wide world of speed. Not those who have known what it is to enter that world, where dream and reality meet as sweetly as a red leather ball coming off the middle of a well-oiled bat. But these players do not resemble the lucky ones who have heard that sweet sound. As he begins to distinguish the individual faces in the group he picks out Worrell at its centre. And the first thing he notices is that he looks tired. As he walks across the open space in front of Michael to the practice nets, Worrell looks like a man with very few steps left in him. Like a man who has in him only those steps required to get him through the day, before he sits down and closes his eyes for a very long time. While Michael is contemplating this, the door beside the Members Stand opens a second time and two more players step out into the morning sunshine. The shorter one he doesn't immediately place, but there is no mistaking the gleaming, golden crucifix that hangs round the neck of Wesley Winfield Hall. One of those to whom speed comes as naturally and easily as a grin.

Whether it is simply the way he is looking at things, or that the players are simply so tired that they are moving ever so slowly, he doesn't know. But they seem to be passing across in front of him for far, far longer than the journey from the dressing rooms to the nets should really take. And during this dreamy procession he seems to have ample time to reach into his school bag and remove a pen and a scrap of paper — some unread, anonymous notice from the previous day's school — and hold it into the air. This sudden movement disturbs the quiet calm of the morning and the players turn as one towards the source of the disturbance and see a tall teenage boy in his grey school uniform holding a scrap of white paper aloft. The group halts as one, Michael steps forward and watches in silence as the paper and the pen are passed round and the entire team signs the blank side of the school notice.

Throughout, nobody speaks. And it is only as he steps back a pace, while the group is still standing as one before him, that he feels the need to respond. Feels that he can't simply stand there in that tremendous silence and let the moment pass without comment. But he can think of nothing to say that might be compressed into the few words there is time for. And in the same instant it occurs to him that a gesture — not words — is required. That it is only through gesture that he can speak as quickly as he must. And, without knowing why, without having time to weigh up the wisdom of the action, he feels his feet coming together and the rest of his body snapping to attention as he would at school assembly. At the same moment his right arm rises, his open hand is lifted to his brow, and he offers his salute to the quiet group of players miraculously assembled in front of him. And it is at that point, while the rest of the group is looking quizzically at the boy, that the tired frame of Frank Worrell, who seems only to have a few steps left in him, stands to attention at the centre of the group and returns the gesture. He has no sooner lowered his arm than his tired face breaks into a grin as crisp as the morning sun, and he and his team are gone.

Suddenly everything is that much faster. The procession has passed, a crowd has gathered at the practice nets, and the familiar *clock clock* of bat and ball punctuates the gathering sound of traffic and trains. And as Michael folds the school notice and places it back in his bag, he knows that this is as near as he will ever get to that world he once imagined as his. It passed before him, this world, and was then gone, pausing just long enough for Michael to glimpse what they have become — those for whom dream and reality have merged, but who have forgotten in their tiredness that this has happened.

49

Frank Worrell Sheds His Loneliness

Amid the swirling hum of the arena, the crackle of the loudspeakers and the metallic rattle of applause, Frank Worrell is alone. He has been alone throughout the summer. But now he is at the point of shedding his loneliness. It is late in the afternoon, the match is completed, the series over. The crowd — men in suits, women in floral hats and best dresses, boys and girls in school uniforms — fills the arena. In the years to come more people will claim to have been here on this afternoon at the MCG than could possibly have been. But, in a sense, it is true, and in a sense it will be right for everyone to say they were there the day Frank Worrell shed his loneliness.

He is alone when the metallic rattle of applause ceases. He is still alone when the slight figure of Bradman steps up to the microphone with a trophy in his hand, while the Australian captain stands beside him in the shadows of the stand — the Australian captain, whose eyes miss nothing, and whose eyes are still on duty even though the tour is over. And even when Worrell steps to the microphone and is stopped before he can speak by a chorus of song and three loud, emphatic cheers that could be heard for miles outside the ground on this calm summer afternoon, he has still not shed his loneliness.

But when he finally speaks his voice is fragile in a way that it has not been all summer. His words are good, delivered with all the grace of a perfect stroke, one that is written into a moment and brings to the world the distracting beauty of a perfect act. But the voice is fragile. It is fragile because the loneliness is leaving him. And as he speaks to the crowd, the loneliness departs, word by word. But it does not finally leave him until he turns to the Australian captain, his offerings in hand. The captain's cap, which he hands to Benaud, is, he says, his scalp. The small white necktie that follows, his neck. His deep crimson blazer, the upper half of his body. He does not offer the lower half of his body because his legs are too tired to be of use to anyone. Frank Worrell

323

hands the items to the Australian captain. And this, written into the moment and there for all to recall forever after, throughout all the summers that will follow, is his final gift. The gift of grace. He hands them all to the Australian captain, then steps back into the shadows of the stand from which he emerged. With the cap, the scarf and the blazer, he is also handing over the weight of the summer, that part of him that couldn't be shared — until now. As the weight of the cap, scarf and blazer leave him, so too does the loneliness.

He wears a sunny smile, his eyes bright with the moment, lightly touching the rows upon rows of faces that stare back at him from this concrete and steel city-within-a-city. Frank Worrell is no longer alone. The weight he carried all through the summer is off his shoulders.

50.

A Self-Taught Woman

In the evening Michael sits in the kitchen, upright in his chair, mindful of his back. She has the voice of the self-taught, this grandmother he barely knows and who he has barely noticed throughout the summer. He heard the voice of the self-taught often when his father's driver friends came to dinner. It is the way they pronounce certain words, words they get all wrong because they have only ever read them in books or journals and never actually heard them pronounced the way they ought to be. And as he sits listening to his grandmother, Michael reflects that they are all of an age and a type, the self-taught, and for all their knowledge, they always betray themselves.

She is used to commanding the attention of a room, he can see that. And with that nose, that jaw and those eyes (in which he sees the face of his father, and possibly himself), he can see that she was born to. She might well have commanded a lot more than the attention of a room had the times into which she was born not made her one of the self-taught who always betray themselves.

Her bedroom smells of age and her legs and hands are weak. But the twinkle hasn't left her eyes. That will be the last thing to go. And although she is weak, she has dragged herself from her room so that she might talk with everyone, and although the twinkle hasn't left her eyes, the effort of dragging herself here is visible. She is tired, that deep tiredness that even other people can feel. But she is here in defiance of her tiredness, a cool beer in her hand. The day before she couldn't raise her head from her pillow. Tonight she has mustered all the life left in her just to be in the company of people. And although her voice is weak, she talks and talks, about everything — the prime minister's eyebrows, the summer cold that won't go away, the awful whack young Michael's cricket ball makes against the back fence. Why does he do it? she asks as if he's not in the kitchen, addressing herself to Michael's mother and the woman from the house behind theirs, whose shared fence he shatters and who has been coming to the house in the evenings lately because she is a nurse and she knows a few things. Although nobody says what these things are, everybody knows. And his grandmother's eyes, the eyes that look lost but which miss nothing, settle on this woman who has been coming to the house lately, and those eyes know exactly why she's here. Even if she does keep up the game, saying she can't understand for the life of her why this woman, Dorothy, Dot to her friends, should bother coming by. All this fuss for a simple summer cold. There are sick people out there, she adds. Those eyes that miss nothing soften as she looks upon Michael, seated at the same table, and asks why he does it. And even though she asks the whole room with a smile in her eyes, it's important to her, and she asks again and again, as if the boy were a riddle and the key to solving him were to be found in knowing why he bangs that ball against the back fence, day in day out. She passes from topic to topic, sipping from her beer with tremulous lips, but always returns to the same question. Nobody can tell her why to her satisfaction, least of all the boy himself. He is her riddle, and riddles don't talk, she says with a laugh.

It is not long before Dot addresses the grandmother by her name, in the casual–familiar way of an old friend. Mary, she says, it's your bedtime. And Mary looks at the clock and laughs. She laughs saying that if she thinks this is her bedtime, then she doesn't know her. She, Mary, is famous for seeing everybody out. Isn't she? She turns to Rita for confirmation and Rita nods more than she really needs to, and Michael can see that even now his grandmother is still a powerful woman. Powerful enough to have his mother nodding in agreement with her just a bit too eagerly and just a bit more than is necessary, and powerful enough to play games with this nurse, who clearly knows her way round difficult customers.

But she is not powerful enough to resist the summons to bed because she knows it is right. She might once have seen everybody out, but not now, and she eventually rises from her seat with a feigned air of reluctance that barely masks her exhaustion and relief. For the comfort of bed, at this moment, is what she craves. Before departing she studies the room closely and everyone in it, her eyes lingering on each of them, one by one. She declines Dot's offer to support her arm, and she walks to her room, back straight, head high, carrying the embroidered doily she uses to cover her chamber-pot.

But as straight as her back may be, and as high as her head might be, she will not emerge from that room again. Even as she walks to it, she realises in some part of her that it is more than sleep she craves. And when Rita takes her a small cup of beer later that night, Mary's face has visibly shrunken, as if sucked in, and she can barely lift the head that she held so high just a few hours before. She can only take a few sips before allowing her head to sink back, deep, deep into the soft-piled pillows beneath her. And as her head sinks into those soft, cotton-covered clouds, there is a delicious sense of falling that she can't resist any longer.

She will lie in that room, drifting in and out of sleep, all through the next morning and afternoon. In the cool of the evening, while Vic instructs at the Railway Institute, Black will join Rita and together (the matter out of human hands), they will look on as the Distinguished Guest enters the room. His invitation will be offered, the struggle will be short, and the old woman's decline as dramatic as he suspected. And as he watches, as life is wrenched from her, as the brute fact of the Distinguished Thing at work reveals itself divested of all the fancy talk, he will note as he always does that the body dies hard and that the Old Master may have got it right after all.

51.

A Bad Time to be Talking

The house is quiet. Not because the television and radio have been silenced, or because the family that lives inside has stepped out for a stroll in the soft summer night. Or because those who live inside have long since ceased to have anything much to say to each other. No, the house is quiet in the way that houses are when something has left it and silence has settled on the house in the same way that mourning settles on the shoulders of those who are left behind when someone dies. Black has gone. Rita sits motionless in the kitchen.

When the front door opens out onto the street it does so slowly, so as not to disturb the dead, and shock them back into life. A man in a checked summer shirt, Richard (Dick to his friends), husband of Dot, steps across the lawn in front of the lounge room and onto the gravel driveway.

It is late, still warm, and he walks the length of the street, past the Englishman's house (where George Bedser lives in quiet retirement from work and the world), and on to the main street of the suburb that leads up to the station. To his right, in the streets that run off the main road, the Girls' Home is quiet and empty and the tennis courts lie still in the night in readiness for the following morning. He is the only figure on the street, everything is still and heavy, the entire suburb is in deep mid-week sleep, and for a time he feels as though he is wading through a dream. The feeling that the world is unreal is nothing new to this man because he believes in another one. A better one. He attends his local church every morning, he prays every day. God, prayers, something else beyond all this. He believes it all and he is comfortable with this feeling that the world — its houses, streets, suburbs and cities — is unreal. It reaffirms his faith, his belief that there really is something else out there besides what you see. So when the trick solidity of the world dissolves like an ice-cream in the sun, he is comfortable with the feeling.

He passes the war memorial and the flour mills and eventually comes to the asphalt path that leads up to the railway station. The ticket office is closed, there is no one else about and he stands in the blue shadows of the Arrivals platform, waiting for the 9.50 p.m. from the city that will be carrying Vic home from one of the night classes that he occasionally takes at the old yards.

Soon he sees the yellow headlights of the old red rattler coming towards him up the incline leading from the preceding suburb. He has often heard this train on clear summer nights lying in bed, but he has never seen it. It has always sounded like an empty train, but as it pulls into the platform he sees that it is not. The red wooden carriage doors are flung open, snapped shut, and soon there are three people walking towards him. He sees Vic immediately, his shoulders hunched, his body leaning forward.

'Dick.'

It is neither a question nor a greeting, but an observation. A simple statement of fact. However tired he might be after three hours of explaining the inner workings of the Westinghouse brake to trainee drivers, Vic's eyes are suddenly alert and scared, for there is no good reason why his neighbour should be standing at the ticket gate to greet him at this hour on a Wednesday evening. But the look on his neighbour's face says it all. Vic could ask him what he is doing here, but he skips all that.

'Mum?'

The other passengers have gone. The two men are alone on the platform and Vic watches as his neighbour closes his eyes and nods. He had come to break the news to Vic and along the way had gone over in his mind what he might say. But, in the end, he said nothing. Shortly afterwards they leave the platform and the two men walk back through the dreamy suburb in silence.

In the house he meets Rita's eyes and without speaking to anybody, drops his bag at his feet, walks towards the room that has been his mother's for the last month and ever so quietly opens, then closes the door behind him.

She doesn't look alive, but she doesn't look bad. This is what frightened him most as he closed the door and approached the bed. That she might be a stranger to him, a face made unrecognisable by it all. But she's not. And with the summer, and the night still hot, her hand is warm as he holds it. And although he knows she won't suddenly speak to him of some minor, niggling matter that crossed her mind a few days before, she's not lost to him either. Not yet. She is still sufficiently with him to talk to, and sufficiently gone for him to see it.

There are no tears, there is no great flood of memories, there is barely any feeling. His mind is blank the way it always was after a long shift. There is just this, this fact that she is gone. And not *anywhere*, so that you might feel comforted that some part of her has gone on. No, there is none of that. There is just this simple, enormous fact that she is gone. He's never been able to stuff that simple fact into his brain — that people go and don't come back — and he always thought that at times such as these he might be able to. But instead his mind drifts back to the demonstration brake that he had lectured on that evening, the tea break, the killing of time before they could start again, and it occurs to him that it must have been while he was pulling the brake apart earlier that evening in the Railway Institute classroom, that it happened. While his mind was occupied with the intricacies of the task at hand, of dismantling and reassembling the entire brake system. It was a pleasant time, and it was pleasing the way all the parts fitted back together. That and the sweet breeze that came in over the South Dynon yards and in through the open windows.

It doesn't take long to put all this together, a second or two. He doesn't dwell on it. Nor does he feel he had no right to take pleasure in those few hours in the classroom, during which he imagined that in another life he might well have enjoyed being a teacher, and might well have been a good one.

Over the next hour that he sits with her — this woman who took the roll of notes they pushed onto her, who took her son with her wherever she went and against all advice, but who took him nonetheless because they both had no one else in the world but each other, who took all the stupid, funny looks, and gave him a place in life when he would have had none — over the next hour that he sits with her he is still unable to stuff that simple, enormous fact into his head. That the thing that was her, the spirit that stood up against the whole rotten, bloody bunch and kept her boy when everybody told her to farm him out, has gone. Ma, Mama, Mother. Gone. And as much as he needs to stuff this simple fact into his head, he can't. And so, when he finally leaves the room, when he finally closes the door behind him, after sitting with the corpse of his mother for over an hour, there is some absurd part of him that is still carrying on as though he is simply saying goodnight.

From his spot deep in the backyard where Michael has shattered the fence, Vic can see that the lights in his neighbours' house are still on. Not friends, he notes, but good people. Good enough to help them through what had to be got through. Their jobs done, they have retired to their house, to their children, their children's pets, the mess in the kitchen that hasn't been cleaned up because they've let it slide. And so, he notes, things go on. He nods to himself, acknowledging the inevitability of it. That while some of us pause for death, life moves on.

Rita emerges from the shadows of the apricot tree in the centre of the yard and stops next to him. She'd touch him, but he doesn't want to be touched. Nor does she say anything; he'll talk when he wants.

He looks round from the fence and the lights of his neighbours' house.

'Her struggles are over now.'

He's pretty sure they're the first words he's spoken since getting in. Not much, five words. If he could, he'd take them back. Anybody could have said them, about anybody else. She wasn't just anybody else, but he's using words that anybody could. Yet, as much as he wants better ones, he knows that he meant exactly what he said. And for the moment, that's enough. It's a bad time to be talking. Whatever you say, you're going to regret it. You're going to wish you'd said something better, rather than something that you meant.

They walk back to the house together, through the shadows of the apricot tree, past the passionfruit and the plums, and Vic momentarily wonders what on earth the time might be as he checks out the stars before the flyscreen door closes quietly behind him.

* * *

Vic's mother will lie in her bed until the next afternoon, when the long, black funeral car will come for her. This funeral car will be hours late, and the sealed room in which she lies, in the February heat, will be heavy with the smell of death — the sheets, bed, floor, those wondrous white walls and the windows. And when they have taken her and she is gone, the room will be stripped and washed. All of it. The windows will be left open in that February heat until the funeral a few days later, when the soap, the disinfectant and the wind have done their job and the smell is gone.

Finale

City of Melbourne, 17TH February 1961

'... a gesture spontaneous and in cricket without precedent, one people speaking to another ...'

CLR James, *Beyond a Boundary*

'Never has it been more apparent that the game is greater than the result than in Melbourne on 17 February 1961. Commerce in this Australian city stood almost still as the smiling cricketers from the West Indies, the vanquished not the victors, were given a send-off the like of which is normally reserved for royalty and national heroes.'

Wisden

52.

Finale

Everywhere, everyone, along with their best clothes, has brought the best of themselves. The city is wonderfully strange. Where is the street? Where are the footpaths, the familiar shopfronts and doorways of the everyday world? Michael can see nothing but people, dressed in their best summer clothes as if for a party, for church or some family celebration.

Along Swanston Street the police, in their white summer helmets, hold the crowds back as the slow procession of cars passes through the thin strip of cleared road. Women in floral dresses and floral summer hats blow kisses, men and boys in suit trousers and starched white shorts wave or simply stand and stare at this slowly moving cavalcade.

Above them all, streamers fall from the sky, from the open windows of the buildings looking over the street where office workers wave small flags and let fall from their fingers the ticker-tape of shredded newspapers and magazines.

Michael is standing in the thick swaying crowd on the footpath opposite the Town Hall. This procession, which has brought the residents of the city's suburbs out of their lounge rooms and streets and shops and clubs, is slowing down at the Town Hall entrance. And as it slows down the players, sitting up on the back seats of open cars, open to the streamers and the sun and the pale-blue sky, come into clear view.

Behind his dark glasses Frank Worrell is crying. Michael had not thought he'd see Frank Worrell crying when he woke this morning. But you can see he's crying because he is constantly wiping the tears from his face, and for a long time Michael ignores the other players as he can see only the crying face of Frank Worrell behind his dark glasses. And even when he stops wiping the tears away, Michael knows that he's still crying. It's not that the tears have stopped, it's simply that he has given up wiping them away. He is light, this Frank Worrell. He has shed the weight that he carried all summer, and with the weight he has shed the loneliness. Now he is light, and with every tear that he wipes or fails to wipe from his face, he feels his lightness and is uplifted by it as he reaches out for a shred of confetti fluttering down towards him. Just behind Worrell, the dark-blue suit of Alf Valentine is covered in bright-red lipstick kisses, and he wears his kisses as if they were medallions.

The tired looks of a few days before gone from their faces, the players step from their cars — from the bright sun shower of streamers and coloured tape — into the pillared shade at the entrance to the Town Hall. One by one they gather, a team, before disappearing up the wide, marble steps and into the Town Hall itself. For those few moments that they are gone from view, the street is silent, the flags in the office windows cease fluttering, the streamers pause in mid-fall, and everything is still as the eyes of the crowd turn to the balcony. Slowness falls upon them all. The ticker-tape floats on invisible currents as if it will never touch ground. Heads, arms and hands are at various phases of beginning and completing impossibly drawn-out gestures, and the very sound of the day is delayed on lazy summer waves out beyond the city. This slowness that is falling upon them, this clearing in the cluttered rush of the day, opens for inspection the passing moment, and, while the hands of the Town Hall clock slow to a crawl, for all the world resisting time itself, Michael is held in its thrall.

Then it is gone, this glimpse of slowness, of the moment, and when the players emerge from the shadows of the building it seems to Michael that they are less human and more distant than at any other time that summer. Their eyes are alight, their faces shine all along the wide, grey balcony. They are, indeed, the ones who have been lifted up and swept away from their streets and towns and into that pure world of speed and rhythm and action. With their smiles that speak of faraway lands, they wave to the crowds below on the street, to the crowds hanging from the windows of the Manchester Unity opposite the Town Hall, and even, for all Michael knows, to the crowds they can't see out there in the suburban depths of the city, where, at this moment, the room that was once Michael's is being cleansed, the grandmother he barely knew having been removed from the house. These farewell waves may, for all he knows, extend that far.

Green city trams jingle their bells as they pass through the narrow strip of the street the police have cleared; the cars that follow sound their horns and a part of the crowd beside Michael is suddenly singing.

Will ye nay come back again?

He didn't notice when they started, or if they started at once or if one voice only had started them off and they all became a spontaneous chorus. But the crowd and their song, the jingling trams and car horns, fill the street and float upwards to the pale-blue summer sky. And all of it is music, an accompaniment to this song, its words drifting through the air and echoing down the deserted, honeycomb network of cool, dark arcades that lie behind the city's streets.

Will ye nay come back again?

It is an old song, or it must be an old song, for Michael has never heard it before. But the crowd knows it, and they are singing loudly, unreservedly and unself-consciously in perfect unison. And it occurs to Michael that he has never heard singing in these streets before, let alone singing such as this. And it further occurs to him that these people have never in their lives sung like this, that some part of each of them has waited a lifetime just for this moment when they could release themselves into song and sing like they have never sung before. To be seen singing old songs in public places is not the usual practice of these people. Michael knows this with absolute certainty, because, at the age of sixteen, he may not know many things, but he knows his city and he knows the people who live in it. Today they have found their voice and they have found their song — this brooding, Scottish-sounding thing about coming back again. They will remember, each of them, on some dull distant day given over to remembering, the day they found their voice, found their song and sang it without restraint. And while they are singing, the waving hand of Wesley Winfield Hall stops, and he leans towards that part of the crowd from which the song is rising, and he listens as if hearing the ghosts of his Scottish past singing back to him across the years. And for a moment, the same song flows through them all like the same blood.

Amid the lines of jingling-jangling trams, the hooting cars, the singing, the streamers and shredded strips of newspaper and magazines that are falling from the sky, everybody is waving. It is a way of speaking. The singing, the waving, the just being here — it's all a way of speaking. And as Michael raises his arm he knows he is not just waving goodbye to the figures on the balcony of the Town Hall, but the whole summer — this summer and all the summers, all the years, months, days and hours he spent chasing speed but never catching it. In the end this is as close as he gets. Staring up with the crowd and waving goodbye to the world that he could once have imagined as his, if only and if only and if only.

Yet even as he waves, he knows it's all right. And he doesn't know where this feeling of it being all right comes from. But it's there, whether in the singing, the song, or the city itself that is now so wonderfully strange. For he has been close to it all afternoon, he has seen it and brushed with it, this world of speed, and now, at last, he can let it go. And besides, he's happy to be part of this crowd, who, along with their best clothes, have brought the best of themselves.

The usual, quiet rhythms of the Old Wheat Road prevail. The newsagent waves to the chemist as he carries the evening papers into the shop. The bicycle repair shop owner, the butcher and the greengrocer are all inside their shops and the twilight commerce of the suburb goes on unseen. Only Nat, the barber, leaning against the lollipop stick at the front of his shop, a tailor-made cigarette wedged into his peanut teeth, is out to catch the changing colours of the street.

The carnival has come and gone, its music — those Saturday-night xylophones, tin drums and island voices — already fading. The street is closing back in on itself, and the procession that day, like the whole of the summer, will soon be remembered like a party at which everybody went slightly mad for a short time and about which everybody feels slightly silly afterwards.

Except that something is still there that wasn't before. The rhythms of the street have returned and life goes on as if nothing has happened, but something has. Michael can't point to it, or touch it or picture it, but it's there. Something happened over the summer, and everybody knows it happened. And no matter how much they try to return to the ordinary rhythms and rituals of the street, there will always be a trace of something left over that wasn't there before. Because of this they will always be haunted by the knowledge that, for a while, they were just that bit better than they thought they were.

And the light, slanting across the shopfronts and rooftops, piercing the venetian blinds of all the lounge rooms beyond the street, is a different light. It is part of the something that is still there and which won't go away. For Michael, standing at the top of the Old Wheat Road, with the flour mill and the railway station just behind him, there will always be a trace of this summer left behind. Something you can't point to or touch or neatly frame. But it's there all right, and once it's been it doesn't go away; this vague, nagging feeling that we all just might be a bit better than we thought we were.

Acknowledgements

Many thanks to the following for their help during the writing of this novel:

The Australia Council for a New Work Grant (Established Writers) in 2002 and a six-month residency at the Australia Council's Keesing Studio, Paris, in 2003.

Warwick Franks, former editor of *Wisden*, Australia, for reading the manuscript and for his advice.

Shona Martyn, Linda Funnell, Rod Morrison and Vanessa Radnidge at HarperCollins, and my agent Sonia Land, for their support and enthusiasm.

Finally, my special thanks to Fiona Capp for her constant help, suggestions and advice during the writing of the book. And to Leo — the lion-hearted boy.

STEVEN CARROLL

The Time We Have Taken

Winner of the 2008 Miles Franklin Literary Award

That exotic tribe was us. And the time we have taken, our moment.

1970, Glenroy. One summer's morning Rita is awakened by a dream of her husband, only to look out on an empty bed. It's been years since Vic moved north and left her life, but her house holds memories and part of her remains tied to a different time. As their son Michael enters the tender and challenging realm of first love, he too discovers that innocence can only be sustained for so long.

As they prepare to celebrate Glenroy's 100th anniversary, the residents of the Melbourne suburb look back on an era of radical change. The time has come for them to consider the real meaning of progress — both as a community and in their personal lives.

The Time We Have Taken is a powerful and poignant look at the extraordinary that lies within the ordinary, from a writer of breathtaking prose.

'A writer worth cherishing. His prose is unfailingly assured, lyrical, poised.'
AUSTRALIAN

STEVEN CARROLL

The Art of the Engine Driver

Shortlisted for the Miles Franklin Literary Award

'A veritable little gem ... a beautiful discovery'
ELLE FRANCE

There they are, still as a photograph, listening for the distant thud of the sun as it prepares to drop from the sky ...

On a hot summer's night, a family of three go to a party in their bristling suburbia. But nothing is as it seems and soon we are walking with them through the past lives of a bully, a drunk and a disaffected youth.

As the story of the neighbourhood unfolds the old and the new, diesel and steam, town and country all collide – and nobody will be left unaffected.

The Art of the Engine Driver is a luminous and evocative take on ordinary suburban lives told with an extraordinary power and depth

'... a little masterpiece'
HESSISCHE ALLGEMEINE

'Subtle, true and profoundly touching ... from the first lines of this very beautiful novel by Steven Carroll, an indefinable charm is at work'
LE MONDE

CRAIG SILVEY

Jasper Jones

Winner of the Indie Book of the Year Award 2009

Jasper Jones has come to my window. I don't know why, but he has. Maybe he's in trouble. Maybe he doesn't have anywhere else to go.

Late on a hot summer night at the tail end of 1965, Charlie Bucktin, a precocious and bookish boy of thirteen, is startled by a knock on his window. His visitor is Jasper Jones. Rebellious, mixed-race and solitary, Jasper is a distant figure of danger and intrigue for Charlie. So when Jasper begs for his help, Charlie eagerly steals into the night by his side, terribly afraid but desperate to impress.

Jasper takes him to his secret glade in the bush, and it is here that Charlie bears witness to a horrible discovery. In this simmering summer where everything changes, Charlie learns to discern the truth from the myth.

By turns heartbreaking, hilarious, tender and wise, *Jasper Jones* is a novel to treasure.

'*Jasper Jones confronts inhumanity and racism, as the stories of Mark Twain and Harper Lee did . . . Silvey's voice is distinctive: astute, witty, angry, understanding and self-assured.*'
WEEKEND AUSTRALIAN

'*Impossible to put down . . . There's tension, injustice, young love, hypocrisy . . . and, above all, the certainty that Silvey has planted himself in the landscape as one of our finest storytellers.*'
AUSTRALIAN WOMEN'S WEEKLY

RACHEL HEATH

The Finest Type of English Womanhood

'Heath combines imaginative, fast-paced storytelling with an unerring sense of
period, place and mood ... an exceptionally well-written, suspenseful novel'
GUARDIAN

It is 1946, and seventeen-year-old Laura Trelling is stagnating in
her dilapidated Sussex family home, while her eccentric parents
slip further into isolation. A chance encounter with Paul Lovell
offers her the opportunity to alter the course of her destiny –
and to embark on a new life in South Africa.

Many miles north, sixteen-year-old Gay Gibson is desperate to
escape Birkenhead. When the girls' paths cross in Johannesburg,
Laura is exposed to Gay's wild life of parties and inappropriate
liaisons. Each in her own world, but thrown together, the girls find
their lives inextricably entangled, with fatal consequences ...

'Excellent on the atmosphere of post-war Britain and the lure of South Africa ...
compellingly told, reminiscent of early Doris Lessing   the twists keep the
reader glued to the novel'
INDEPENDENT

'The writing is strong and when the girls' paths become entwined it is
thrillingly macabre'
DAILY TELEGRAPH

PATRICK LANE

Red Dog, Red Dog

*'A shock of a novel; immaculately crafted, deeply thoughtful,
and with a broken-hearted wisdom.'*
JON MCGREGOR

An epic novel of unrequited dreams, Red Dog, Red Dog unfolds over the course of one week in and around a small town in British Columbia in 1958.

Elmer Stark is a violent and distant husband to the increasingly isolated Lillian, but their sons are bound together by the secrets of their childhood years. As Eddy speeds along a reckless path, Tom tries to make sense of their past. Then one night Eddy goes too far, and a dramatic spiral of events is set in motion . . .

Told in part by one of the infant daughters Elmer has buried, Red Dog, Red Dog is a searing novel about hardship and loss, revenge and loyalties.

'This impressive tale of redneck life in British Columbia exudes suffering and menace'
FINANCIAL TIMES

'Lane's exquisite craftsmanship is on display . . . particularly his unerring instinct for images that wound and enlighten in equal measure'
GLOBE AND MAIL